T0159225

Bobo

From Pit to Pinnacle

Doyle Johnson

authorHOUSE®

AuthorHouse™
1663 Liberty Drive
Bloomington, IN 47403
www.authorhouse.com
Phone: 1-800-839-8640

Published by AuthorHouse   07/18/2012

ISBN: 978-1-4772-1216-5 (sc)
ISBN: 978-1-4772-1215-8 (e)

Library of Congress Control Number: 2012909588

Any people depicted in stock imagery provided by Thinkstock are models, and such images are being used for illustrative purposes only.
Certain stock imagery © Thinkstock.

This book is printed on acid-free paper.

Because of the dynamic nature of the Internet, any web addresses or links contained in this book may have changed since publication and may no longer be valid. The views expressed in this work are solely those of the author and do not necessarily reflect the views of the publisher, and the publisher hereby disclaims any responsibility for them.

CHAPTER 1

It was August 26, 1929 in rural Arkansas, Robert Harrel was born. For a time it wasn't certain the woman would be able to deliver the child; but eventually she did. He weighed in at an astounding 14 pounds, 6 ounces and was 24 inches long. He was, to say the least, an unusual child. The doctor told the woman he would most likely be somewhat retarded and difficult to teach.

On the birth certificate the father was listed as 'unknown'. The mother was well known for her promiscuity, sometimes entertaining several different men in a single night; besides that, she wasn't the brightest bulb in the chandelier.

The boy grew much faster than normal and was grossly neglected, even as a baby. Very rarely was he held and often cried for long periods of time. Even feeding was done at his mother's convenience. Compounding the problem, she was abusive, often treating him with disdain, creating in him a massive inferiority complex.

The people often referred to him as '*Myrtle's Wonder*', adding '*wonder who his daddy is*'. Others referred to him as '*The Village Idiot*'. Robert could only guess at what *idiot* meant, knowing full well they were making sport of him. When the men folk came, Robert was scolded and told to stay outside the house until he was called.

He'd hear things like, *"Beat it kid, I'm here to see your momma."*

Or *"Scram dummy, if I need you I'll call you."*

Or *"Why don't you go read a book?"*

It was hard for him to understand why no one liked him but came to expect people to say hurtful things to him.

By the time he started to school, he was much larger than the boys his age. Because of that he became the victim of many indignities from those his own age.

The little country school was near the foot of a huge mountain, about a mile from where he lived. A very large oak tree located toward the back of the play ground, near a small creek, provided sanctuary for Robert. The gentle, rippling sound of the water as it flowed over the rocks and the soothing sound of the breeze that caused the trees to move as though they were dancing to its music, helped restore his peace of mind. Each morning you'd see him, with his rag covered lunch, making his way to it.

His first day of school did nothing to dispel the notion that he was slow.

The teacher called the class to order and explained the way they were to introduce themselves and learn the names of the others.

Indicating the row to her left she began to explain: "This is my left," raising her arm, "and this will be row number one," again indicating with her left arm. "Next row to my right will be row two; the next will be row three, and so on until we've finished with introductions. We will begin in the front with the first pupil in row one. She will stand and tell us her first and last name. When she is finished, she'll be seated and the next pupil behind her will stand and do the same. When the last pupil in row one is finished the first pupil in row two will begin. We will begin with me, my name is Eva Cleves; you may call me Ms. Cleves."

When it came Robert's turn, he stood silent for a long time, finally said, "My name is Robert." He continued to stand but said nothing more.

"Robert, what is your last name?" the teacher asked.

Again a long pause, "It's Robert I guess," he said.

A burst of laughter erupted, to which Ms. Cleves pounded the desk and in an affirmative voice declared, "We'll have no such outbursts!"

Again turning her attention to Robert, asked, "Robert, what is your daddy's name?"

Another long pause, "It's daddy I guess."

Again the class snickered, and again Ms. Cleves admonished them.

She asked Robert to be seated and called on the next pupil to continue the introductions.

The last to stand was a small lad who was physically handicapped with a speech impediment. He rose and said, "My name is Pepe Posey."

Pepe lived with his mother, his dad was killed in a farm accident when he was very young. His mother, a proud woman, always recognizing Pepe's handicap, never allowed him the luxury of self-pity. Instead, she was careful to instill in him a sense of pride and self-confidence.

"Pepe, you can be anything you want to be! Only your mind will keep you from achieving your goals, not your handicap. It's your body that has the handicap, not your mind; never let your body rule your mind. This was my approach to life when your father was killed. Times were very hard then. No one had money and there were no jobs, but I never stopped believing. I was more fortunate than many, I found a job and was able to provide for us. There will be up and downs in your life: use the ups to prepare for the downs; use the down as a learning experience. Bad things soon pass; good things appear from sources we are unable to see or anticipate."

On the play ground, the children followed Robert around, antagonizing him. The younger ones would run up behind him and poke a finger in his back, then run away laughing;

The larger ones would say things like: *"My name is Robert Robert I guess."* or *"My daddy's name is daddy."* or *"How'd you get so smart Robert? I bet my daddy can whip your daddy daddy."*

Robert would run from them but they'd follow and continue humiliating him.

He would sometimes miss class altogether, just sit by the tree and doodle. The faculty, aware of his situation, didn't complain but considered him something of an outcast. Robert was aware he was not thought of as a part of the class, he was never asked a question, or asked to be part of a class function.

Because of Pepe's mother's teaching, it was a natural thing for him to be greatly troubled by the way other people treated Robert. Finding him sitting behind a tree crying, he said, "Bobo, (Pepe's way of pronouncing Robert) would you be my friend?"

"No! No one wants to be my friend, I ain't good like other people; my Mommy told me so."

"I want to be your friend," Pepe said. "I think you're better'n them others."

"If I'm good like other kids, why do they laugh at me?" Robert asked.

"Maybe they don't know you're good like them. They laugh at me 'cause I walk and talk funny. But you and me could be friends! Me and you!!" Pepe said. "Friends forever! This could be our very own big tree."

"Am I good like you?" Robert asked.

"Bobo, you're good as anyone in the whole world!"

The old tree was in proximity to a hole in the fence behind the school which, with great difficulty for Robert, provided access to the creek. Sometimes Robert and Pepe would sneak through the fence and watch the fish, frogs and small snakes. The huge mountain lay in the back ground.

Once, while visiting the tryst, Robert asked, "Pepe, do you think frogs and fish and snakes are friends with each other?"

"Yeah, I think they are! They don't fight each other," said Pepe.

"I like to watch 'em. Can we be friends with them?" Robert said.

"Yeah sure! They're afraid of us at first, but after a while, if we be good to them, they begin to like us. Most animals like to eat 'cause they ain't got nobody to bring 'em food." Pepe continued, "If we bring 'em food, they'll be our friends."

The boys grew silent, each engrossed in his own thoughts, imagining all the possibilities the woods and the mountain had to offer.

As the day grew long Pepe said, "I have to go home now, Mommy will be worried about me."

"I reckon my mom wouldn't miss me if I didn't come home. She jist wouldn't have nobody to hit around," Robert said, and reluctantly began to make his way home, knowing full well how things would be there.

"Where've you been?" she yelled as he sauntered into the house. "And don't give me any of you crazy excuses. You'll never be worth 2 cents," and slapped the back of his head as he walked by.

"Mommy, please don't hit me." he said.

"Don't give me any sass or I'll hit you again. Now get on with the chores."

Soon a man came to the house and Robert was told to beat it.

Rejected again, he simply went for a walk.

*

Next day after school, as the boys sat talking at the tree, Bobo told of the man coming to his house and being told to leave, and that he was sure the man had come to see his Momma.

"I didn't have no place to go, I jist walked around for a while until he left."

"Bobo, why don't you come home with me? Momma can fix us supper and you can go home later. That way, you'll know where I live and when you get kicked out, you can come to my house," Pepe said.

"Shoot! Your momma wouldn't want me over to your house," Robert said.

"Sure she would! Come home with me and I'll show you," Pepe said.

Robert sat silent, "Come on Bobo, go home with me; I want you to and Momma will be happy for you to come."

Finally, he decided to go and as they walked along Robert asked, "Are you sure your Momma won't be mad at us?"

"Of course she won't be mad at us; she'll be happy."

After arriving at Pepe's home and inside his mother cheerfully asked, "Pepe! Who's this you have with you?"

Pepe introduced Robert, "Mom, this is my friend I've told you so much about, his name is Robert."

The introduction wasn't necessary, she was aware of this boy's home life as well as his mother's reputation, "Well, Robert, it's so good to finally meet you, my name is Helen Posey, maybe you'd like to call me Ms. Posey."

Amazed at how clean and neat things were in Pepe's house and unaccustomed to someone being nice to him he became very uncomfortable but said nothing. He knew he could never ask Pepe to come to his house for a visit because his house was always dirty and unkempt.

CHAPTER 2

2nd Grade

At the end of the first grade, Robert was the focus of the faculty. At the meeting, his situation was the subject for discussion.

"Robert has a real problem getting along with the other children, there seems to be an uproar when he's in their presence," one member said.

"He certainly doesn't communicate with the others, none seem to want to be friends with him," another said. "Ms. Cleves says he never wants to participate in class activity, but whiles away his time scribbling."

"Nothing can be gained by keeping him in the 1st grade another year; it's obvious he's not capable of being taught at an accelerated pace; we have to do what we can and keep him moving upward," the principal said. "Are there any questions or suggestions that differ from my analysis?"

No one offered.

"Then we promote him to the 2nd grade."

Life was no more pleasant in the 2nd grade than before; the children took every opportunity to poke fun and belittle Robert. A new teacher was just another hurdle for him: a new name (Ms. Tate) to remember; another person

Bobo

unfamiliar with his problems; another person with little patience for him.

On the playground someone would engage Robert in conversation while another would slip up behind him on hands and knees, then the person talking to him would shove him backward causing him to fall sprawling, then everyone would leave running in all different directions.

They would make fun of his clothes, "Are them your Sunday-go-to-meetin' clothes?"

"I bet your work clothes are something to see," another would say.

Still another, "I bet you combed your hair with a garden rake."

The kids would always get a booming laugh from such remarks, making Robert run for the big tree.

Back in the classroom while everyone, including Ms. Tate, was busy at one thing or another, 'Fish', (as he was called), a somewhat well-to-do kid, hit Robert with a 'spit-ball'.

He turned to Fish and looked at him for a long time. Fish looked away as though it wasn't he who had thrown the 'spit-ball'. As soon as Robert looked away, Fish hit him with another one. Ms. Tate, unaware of what was going on, was shocked by what happened next. Robert got up and walk back to Fish, took the spit ball and mashed it on his head.

"Robert!" Tate exclaimed, "get in your seat!"

"He—"

"Get in your seat this instant!"

Walking back to his seat he started to tell her what had happened, but she sternly pointed to his seat. Before sitting down, Robert took one more look at Fish, who was almost laughing out loud; there were smiles on many of the

Doyle Johnson

children. Ms Tate admonished him once again, "Robert! Sit down!"

He sat down with a thud and turned again to look at Fish.

Fish, grinning broadly, pointed his finger toward himself, affirmly nodded his head.

Later, on the play ground, Robert came to Fish and said, "Don't hit me with no more spit balls."

"Whats ya gonna do 'bout it big boy?" was Fish's reply.

Robert grabbed him, threw him to the ground, took his ear and gave a mighty twist, causing him to let out a scream.

Robert let him up and again said, "Don't hit me with no more spitballs and I won't hurt you again."

Fish, running away yelling, "I'm gonna tell the teacher."

When the class came to order, Ms. Tate said, "Robert, come go with me."

Leading the way to the principal's office.

George Fincher was noted for his sternness and strict discipline. He was feared by all who were compelled to appear before him; even the rest of the faculty kept their distance.

Once inside Ms. Tate began, "Mr. Fincher, Robert is accused of hurting another pupil's ear. I've had to sternly reprimand him while class is in session but it doesn't seem to have had an effect."

"What do you have to say for yourself Robert?" the principal asked.

"Fish hit me with a spitball; twice," Robert said.

The principal turned and looked at Ms. Tate, "I didn't see anything like that. The first thing I saw was Robert getting out of his seat, walking back to the seat of the other pupil and mashing a spitball on his head. He had to be admonished three times to return to his seat before he would sit down."

"Robert, do you understand you can't hurt people just because you can?" Fincher said.

"He wouldn't stop hittin' me with them spitballs."

"Ms. Tate says she saw nothing of the sort and I believe her," Fincher said.

"Because you disturbed the class this way, you have to stay in the classroom and miss two recesses. If you hurt someone again, the punishment will be a spanking. Do you understand?"

Not knowing what to say, Robert stood silent.

"Do you understand?" Fincher insisted.

Still Robert said nothing.

Fincher turned to Ms. Tate and said, "Keep me posted."

While the boys continued to play mean tricks on Robert, always making it seem to be he who perpetrated the incident, Robert and Pepe spent a lot of time at the *'Big Tree'* when away from the class room.

Ms. Tate was unaccustomed to students who idled their time away, not completing their assignments. Aware of Robert's potential, she aware of Robert's potential, paid little attention to his scribbling and doodling. A large hole in the side of the *'Big Tree'* provided storage for his pencils and paper, furnished by the school as he never had money. Robert, often scribbling, aroused Pepe's curiosity. However, not wanting to embarrass him, he never asked to see what he was doing.

On one occasion, as they whiled away the day, Robert handed Pepe a sheet of paper and said, "Yesterday I saw this critter; it was the first time I'd seen one like it. Do you know what it is?" he asked Pepe.

Pepe took the paper and cried out, "Holy Cow, Bobo! Did you draw this?"

A drawing of a possum so perfect, it looked like a photograph.

"Yeah, I'm sorry; it looked like that to me," Robert said sheepishly. "You ain't mad at me are you Pepe?"

"My, my, no Bobo, that's good, real good! What else can you draw?"

"I don't know, I can draw what I see," Robert said.

"Can you draw a fox?" Pepe asked.

"Maybe, I saw one getting a drink at the creek one day; I'll show you what it looked like to me," Robert said.

In a few minutes Robert passed Pepe another paper. To his amazement, the drawing revealed an absolutely perfect drawing of a fox drinking at the edge of a creek.

"Bobo, may I have these for my own?" Pepe asked.

"You can have them if you promise not to let anyone else see 'em; ever. They'd laugh at me, and I don't like it when they laugh at me. Don't even tell anyone you got 'em," Robert said.

"I promise I'll keep 'em forever," Pepe said.

Pepe didn't realize what he had just promised Bobo, recognizing the potential of his talent, he was often tempted to tell his mother, but kept his promise to Bobo and did not.

Robert unaware of his talent and so subdued by the treatment he received, not only at school, but at home as well, either hid or discarded his drawings for fear of ridicule.

CHAPTER 3

The Dog

On one of Robert's occasions at the tree, a half grown pup came up to him, sort of cowed down, wagging his tail, wanting to be petted but afraid to be too bold.

"Come on Rocky, come let me see you," Robert said.

Still the pup lay wagging his tail, eyes pleading to be accepted. Robert opened his rag covered lunch, consisting of a piece of cornbread and home made bacon, took a piece of the cornbread and held it out to the pup.

Slowly it began to crawl toward him. Robert picked him up and held him to his chest, immediately the dog began to lick his face and hands. At last Robert had something of his very own that loved him.

"Where'd you come from? You're so pretty, you can be my very own dog, we can be friends."

So began a lasting relationship. He'd sit at the tree for hours, petting Rocky and talking to him as though he were another person.

"Rocky, someday me and you are gonna climb this old mountain; we'll be so high we can feel the clouds. Shoot, I bet we could almost touch the sky. When we get to the top, no one can hurt us."

Each day Robert would bring extra cornbread and bacon and divide with Rocky. Robert felt as comfortable talking to Rocky as he did with Pepe.

Rocky soon learned the school routine and was always there waiting when Robert arrived.

Robert was apprehensive about approaching his mother with the idea of bringing Rocky home but finally got the nerve to take him with him and approached his mother.

"Mom, can I have a dog?" he asked.

"No! You may not have a dog. I can't feed another mouth around here. Besides that's the worst looking thing as I've ever seen!" she said.

"But mom he won't eat much, I'll give him half of mine." Robert argued.

"NO! You can't have that dog and I won't hear another word about it. Now get out of here and take that mongrel with you before I get the broom after the both of you," and gave the dog a kick and shoved Robert out the door.

Disenchanted, and as he sometimes did, Robert sauntered back toward the school house and the tree, taking a discarded piece of carpet and Rocky with him.

Back at the school, Robert fixed Rocky a bed with the piece of carpet and had him lay on it for a while before leaving him.

"Rocky, Mom don't like you, so you have to stay here for now. But don't be afraid, cause she don't like me neither. Me and you, we are friends and we can be together."

Rocky held onto every word as if he completely understood.

Reluctantly Robert started back toward home, looking back, Rocky had begun to follow.

"No, Rocky you can't go with me this time." Turning and pointing to the bed, he led the dog back to his bed, "you have to stay here for now."

Again he turned to leave. Rocky stood watching until Robert had gone quite a distance, then slowly began to follow.

Again Robert took him back to his bed, "Now Rocky, you have to stay here for now."

Robert didn't look back until he had gone a good distance, looking back he saw Rocky curled up on his bed.

Next morning Robert was up early and hurrying toward the school to see if Rocky was O.K. There he was, standing, vigorously wagging his tail but not leaving the bed.

"Come here boy!" clapping his hands, "It's okay, you can come out now."

In two big bounds, Rocky was in Robert's arms.

Robert, anxiously waited for Pepe to get to school so he could show off Rocky.

Pepe was as delighted with the pup as Robert. "Now we have a friend who is a friend of yours and a friend of mine," he said. "Can you draw Rocky?"

"I can show you what he looks like to me," Robert said, and began to draw.

Soon he showed Pepe how Rocky looked to him.

*

On many cloudy days, the top of the mountain couldn't be seen.

"Pepe, do you think we could climb to the top of that mountain?" Robert asked as they sat watching the flow of the creek. Rocky lay nearby, watching the two as though he understood the conversation.

"I think we could, but it might take us a long time," Pepe said.

After dwelling on the idea for a while, Robert said, "Pepe, do you think your legs will get too tired?"

"I betcha I can climb that old mountain just good as you," Pepe said, "but if I tell my Momma, she won't let me do it."

"You could tell her you're going to my house," Robert said. "Someday let's do it. I bet we could see a long way, we might even get as high as the clouds. Someday I wish I could ride on a cloud, they look so soft and fluffy!"

"Silly Bobo, you can't ride on a cloud; you'd fall right through it!"

"Anyway, someday I want to ride on one," Robert said, as his thoughts turned to reality.

"I have to head for home," Pepe said, struggling to get to his feet. "Momma will get mad if I'm very late."

"Sometimes I think my Momma wishes I wouldn't even come home at all," Robert said wistfully.

As Pepe made his way through the fence and across the school yard, Robert became very sad. "Rocky, do you wish other people liked you? I wish people liked me; I wish Momma liked me. Pepe is the only friend I have that can talk to me; you're my friend but you can't talk.

As darkness set in, Robert crawled through the fence and made his way toward home, this time, taking Rocky with him. Afraid to mention him to his Momma, he took him to the little house behind and said goodnight.

CHAPTER 4

3rd Grade

Each day, getting to school was a heavy dread; knowing the only thing awaiting him there was more ridicule; more humiliation.

Ms. Evers was the teacher but seldom paid him any attention at all; even if she asked him a question, he never knew the answer and that just gave the hecklers more material to use against him. Even though he was much larger than the other boys, he never got picked to play on the ball team and because the children laughed and poked fun at him, no one wanted to be his friend. When the loneliness and disappointments became almost unbearable, there was always his true-blue friend Pepe. He knew Robert had something very valuable but didn't know how to bring it out. So, true to his promise, he told no one.

Valentine Day came and all the children exchanged valentines but he got none.

Cherl, a pudgy, but pretty girl, came to him and said, "Robert, I got too many valentines, could you please take one?"

"Shoot! What do I need with an old valentine? I don't know what it says," he said.

"You just read the words," she said

"I don't know how to read," he said.

Holding out several valentines, Cherl said, "You just pick one and I'll read it to you."

Robert just stood, staring at the valentines for a long time, finally picking one with a big red heart which read, ***BE MY VALENTINE.***

Cherl read the words, still Robert just stared, not understanding what it all meant.

Embarrassed, she simply walked away.

Pepe, that old girl tried to give me this (holding out the valentine) I don't know what she meant. She said, 'Be My Valentine.' I don't know, what is a valentine?"

"If someone likes you they might give you a valentine saying, Be My Valentine; that means they want to be your friend."

"Are you my valentine?"

"In a way I am but usually it's boys who give valentines to girls and girls give valentines to boys."

With a puzzled look, he said, "I ain't no valentine." and began to walk away.

"Wait a minute Bobo, maybe she likes you, don't you see?" Pepe said.

Robert was quite sure he didn't want no girl liking him and he didn't want to be anybody's valentine.

4th Grade

By now Robert had developed a deep-seated complex and spent more and more of his time at the tree. His size made him an imposing figure yet the kids continued to torment him. By now, the class had developed the playground bully. Gordon Haley (*Gordy for short*) seemed to have ascended to that dubious distinction.

"Where'd ya git those fine duds, Robert Robert?" Gordy asked.

When Robert didn't respond, Gordy continued to tantalize, "Bet that belt set ya back a bundle; I have one jist like it to tie up my calf," bringing a big round of laughter from the kids around. Still not satisfied, Gordy continued, "Where'd ya git that old hound dog? It shore is ugly!" then reached down and pulled Rocky's ear, causing him to cry out.

Robert, sitting leaned back against the tree, jumped to his feet, grabbed Gordy by his overall bib, pulled his face up close to his own and said, "You hurt Rocky—now I'm gonna hurt you." With that he pushed Gordy back against the tree. A loud groan came from somewhere deep in Gordy's throat. As two of Gordy's friends started toward them, Robert who was still holding Gordy, spun around and shoved him into the approaching duo, causing all three to fall flat on the ground.

By this time, Mr. Fincher, the principal, had seen what was happening and was making his way to the fight. "Who started this?" he asked.

"Robert," the crowd answered.

"Come with me Robert," Fincher said, taking him roughly by the arm and headed for the office.

Once in the office, Mr. Fincher said, in a menacing tone, "Robert, we don't allow fighting on the school ground. You should be ashamed; you are much bigger than the other boys.

We talked about this before; about you being unruly.

The principal paused for a few moments, allowing Robert time to think and then continued; "Its school policy, if someone starts a fight, he must be punished. Bend over and keep your hand on the desk." With that he proceeded to paddle him.

"I didn' do nothin' wrong; I won't come back to this school again. I didn' do nothin' wrong."

With that he ran from the office, back to the tree where he and Rocky went thru the fence, across the stream and they began their way to the top of the mountain.

As they made their way along, Robert continued to talk to Rocky not paying much attention to the direction they were going. After climbing for some time, Robert said to Rocky, "Let's stop for a while, we must be close to the top."

As they sat there, Rocky snuggled in Robert's lap, they both fell asleep. When they awakened, it was almost sundown. Robert stood and said, "Rocky, I don't think we're going to get to the top today, maybe we oughta go back and try again sometime."

As they started back down and daylight began to fade, Robert became disoriented. Part of the time he was going downhill, sometimes uphill, sometimes neither, and soon became exhausted. Again they stopped and fell asleep. When they woke up it was beginning to be daylight. Rocky seemed anxious, his tail wagging feverously, began to run around and around Robert, down the hill a ways and back to Robert again. When Robert got to his feet, Rocky barked just one time and began to trot down hill. Robert was hungry as well as very thirsty. Thinking he had no choice, he followed Rocky, who would stop occasionally, look back at Robert, then turn suddenly and continue down hill.

At last they came to the creek where they eagerly began to drink.

Once again Robert sat down to rest. Still somewhat disoriented, and since there was no sign of the school, he wondered if they should go up stream or down stream. Rocky was content for a little while, but soon began to jump around and when Robert got to his feet; Rocky started upstream and soon arrived at the back of the school. They stopped long enough to drink again, then across the creek, through the fence and on to the school yard.

"Rocky, you're a good dog, we never would've got off that old mountain if you hadn't known the way."

Rocky just looked up at Robert and vigorously wagged his tail.

As he made his way home, he wondered if his mother knew he didn't come home last night. Rocky, seemingly assuming he had found his home with Robert, was happily tagging along. As soon as the woman saw them coming she met them, yelling and screaming, "Where have you been and what have you been up to?" she yelled, "I told you to get rid of that—dog, now you've brought him here."

With that she grabbed a broom and began hitting Rocky, he yelped and began running behind and around Robert. "Momma, don't hurt Rocky, he's a good dog," he said.

Still she continued to beat on Rocky. Finally, Robert took hold of her trying to restrain her but still she resisted. In an effort to free herself from Robert, she tore her dress, fell, skinned her knee and bumped her head as she fell.

"That does it! I've had it with you, you're going to the sanatorium, I can no longer put up with you."

With that she took off toward the neighbors and told her story. She asked the neighbor if he would come and take Robert to the sheriff and ask him to get him to the sanatorium where he can be managed. "He has become violent and I'm afraid he'll hurt me. You can see what he has done to me today simply because I asked him where he was last night."

The neighbor told the woman he wouldn't get involved physically but would drive to town and get the sheriff, and this he did.

When the sheriff arrived, Robert was no where to be found. They searched for a long time before finding he and Rocky hiding behind his favorite place, the old big tree at school.

The sheriff approached him and said, "Robert, your mother has asked me to take you to a new place where you can be safe and have a nice room, warm clothes and good food. Would you like to go there now?"

"I ain't done nothing wrong, my Momma was beating Rocky, he's is a good dog and Momma was hurting him. I asked her to stop but she wouldn't; Rocky is a good dog."

"If you'll just come with me, you can ride in my car. We'll take Rocky and he'll have a good place to stay and he'll get real good food. Would you like that?" the sheriff asked.

"Will they hurt Rocky?" Robert asked.

"No! No one will hurt Rocky and you can see him everyday," the sheriff assured him.

"Will they laugh at me there?" Robert asked. "I don't like for people to laugh at me."

"Oh no, you'll be fine there and you can see your Mom anytime."

"I don't want to see my Mom, she don't like me because I ain't good like other boys," Robert said.

As they drove to Sheriff Mack Haskin's office, not much else was said. When they arrived the sheriff said, "You have to stay here tonight and you can't run away, do you understand?"

"Can Rocky stay with me?" He asked.

"Yes, we'll arrange for him to stay right with you tonight. O.K.?" The sheriff asked.

"If Rocky can stay, I won't run away, Rocky is my friend."

"I imagine a young guy like you must be pretty hungry, how long has it been since you had something to eat?" the Sheriff asked.

"Yesterday morning."

"Someone will bring you something real soon."

"Will they bring enough for Rocky too?" Robert asked.

"Sure, Rocky will be fed as well."

Soon a woman brought Robert and Rocky something to eat.

After finishing the meal and still tired from the excursion on the mountain they both fell asleep.

CHAPTER 5

The Hearing

Next day, after eating again, a man came to Robert's room and told him he was to go with him.

"Can Rocky come with us?"

"No, not this time, he has to stay here, but he'll be fine and we'll be back later today." the man assured him.

Again in the sheriff's car, they soon came to a huge white house with lots of windows. The man stopped the car and they went inside.

As Robert entered the room, he saw his Mom, the principal from school, the sheriff and some of the boys that enjoyed tormenting him. Confused, he sat where he was told and wondered what all this meant. His Mom wouldn't so much as look at him; the principal would occasionally look but when Robert looked at him, he quickly turned away.

Finally a man in a black coat came into the room and everybody stood up, another said, "This hearing is now in session. The case before us is Myrtle Harrell vs Robert Harrell to determine if Robert Harrell, he being somewhat intellectually challenged, is capable of functioning normally in open society.

The complaint states that Robert's actions have become violent at times and Ms. Harrell states she's afraid of him;

that he has assaulted her, torn her dress and caused her to fall, injuring her head. There are other witnesses which will attest to Robert's violent nature."

"I didn't do nothin' wrong; she was hurting my dog," Robert blurted out, to which the man in the black coat told him he wasn't permitted to speak until he was called upon to do so.

"I didn't do nothin' wrong," Robert insisted.

"Ms. Harrell will you take the stand and state your case?" The man said.

She came to the stand, took an oath to tell the truth but still refused to look a Robert.

"Now Ms. Harrell, will you state your reasons for wanting Robert committed to this institution?" the man said.

With her hands in her lap, nervously wringing them, she said, "He's gotten to where he stays out all night, no one knows where he is; he refuses to abide by my rules. This latest event took place after showing up in the early morning, no one knows where he'd been, bringing with him this pitiful looking dog, which he had been told not to do, that we couldn't afford to feed another animal. When I objected to the dog, he grabbed my dress and tore it, throwing me to the ground, injuring my head. I didn't know what to expect, he's so much stronger than me. I am, for the most part, defenseless."

Sitting silent for a moment, she continued, "He won't go to school anymore, I just don't know how to deal with him."

Myrtle grew silent, continued to wring her hands, without looking up.

"Is there anything further you wish to say?" The judge asked.

"No, I reckon not. I just don't know what to do."

"Then you may step down."

"Are there others who would have a say in this matter?" the judge asked.

"Yes sir," the bailiff said, "there are other witnesses who will testify."

"Who is next?" he asked

"Will George Fincher please take the stand?"

"Sir my name is George Fincher; I'm the junior high principal at the school where Robert previously attended. He routinely causes a disturbing atmosphere around the other pupils.

I was witness to him abusing three other children on the play ground and was compelled to discipline him according to school policy. He's so much larger than the other boys, there are none his equal. In this incidence, he threw three boys down, all at the same time, stating they were bothering his dog. He appears to be incapable of interacting with other children his age. I would recommend he be institutionalized."

"Anything further Mr. Fincher?" the judge asked.

"No sir."

"Will Gordy Haley please take the stand." the judge said.

After Gordy was seated in the witness chair, the judge asked, "What do you have to say in this matter?"

"Sir, the incident Mr. Fincher mentioned, occurred as I bent down to pet his little dog and he violently assaulted me. When my friends came to my aid, he threw us all down and no doubt would have continued to do us harm except Mr. Fincher came to our rescue." Gordy declared.

"Were you abusing his dog?"

"No sir, I was just going to pet him," Gordy lied.

"If you have nothing further you may step down."

Pausing briefly, the judge continued, "Robert do you have something to say in this matter?"

"I ain't done nothin' wrong. She was hurting my dog. I asked her to stop and she wouldn't so I got hold of her arm so she'd stop hurtin' him and she jerked away and fell."

"Young man, before you can tell your side, you must be seated in the witness chair" recognizing Robert didn't understand, added, "This chair," indicating with his left arm.

The bailiff took him by the arm and helped him be seated.

"Now you may tell us if what we've heard here in true." The judge said.

He repeated what had been said.

"When you say 'she', are you referring to your mother?"

"Yeah, she was hurting my dog."

"What do you have to say concerning three boys down at school?" The judge asked.

"Gordy was pulling my dog's ears and making him yelp, so I took him by his overall and told him to stop. Two other boys came to help him and I pushed Gordy into them and they fell down."

"Do you want to hurt anyone who bothers your dog?"

"Rocky is my friend; they shouldn' want to hurt him, he's a good dog."

"Robert, do you love your Momma?" He asked

"Momma don't like me so I don't like her back."

The judge, somewhat taken aback, said, "Did it make you mad when your Momma said you couldn't keep the dog?"

"She said we couldn' feed him but I told her I would share my lunch with him, but she just kicked him and pushed me outside."

"If someone was hurting your dog, would you hurt them back?"

"Yes" Robert said.

After a few moments of contemplation, the Judge asked, "Is there anyone here to speak on behalf of Robert Harrel?"

"Yes sir, for the record, my name is Sheriff Mack Haskin; if Robert is to be committed, I promised him his dog would be cared for. Since none of his family wants anything to do with Robert, I recommend we make his dog a ward of the state, that the dog be adequately provided for and Robert be allowed reasonable time to spend with the animal."

"Are there objections to this proposal?" The Judge asked.

There was none.

"Although on the surface, this young man does not appear to be a threat to anyone when left to himself, there is evidence of his propensity toward violence when challenged. Since he has no one willing to assume responsibility for him, and since all the evidence presented here today indicates that this unfortunate lad has become a menace to those around him and with no evidence to the contrary, I have no choice but to make him a ward of the state. I hereby order him committed to the institution indefinitely or until such time he might be re-evaluated and found competent to make sound judgments and provide for himself. At such time, these orders may be set aside. In view of these unusual circumstances, it is further ordered the dog, who answers to the name of Rocky, is to become a ward of the state and be adequately provided for and that Robert be allowed to spend time with the animal as circumstances permit." the Judge declared, "Hearing adjourned."

Staring at his mother, bewildered, as the people began to leave the court room, Robert began to cry, "Momma—MOMMA!!! What does this mean? Why can't I come home with you?"

The woman walked defiantly past Robert without so much as looking at him.

CHAPTER 6

The Sanatorium

After driving to the sanatorium, the matron took Robert by the arm and began to lead him away. Robert began to wail in his booming voice, "I didn't do nothin' wrong, I didn't do nothin' wrong."

"Everything is going to be alright," Pinky Summers, the matron assured him "You will have lots of new friends."

"I want to see Rocky—I want to see Rocky!! The man in the black suit said I could see Rocky, Rocky is my friend," Robert insisted.

"OK, after we get you settled in and you know where your new home is, you can play with Rocky for a while," Pinky assured him.

True to her word, she showed Robert his room and explained the rules, afterwards showing and describing the day room.

"This is where you may spend time writing, playing board-games and the likes. When you need pencils, colors, or paper just ask; we'll get them for you. We have rules and everyone must abide by them so everyone may be safe. If you violate the rules, some of your privileges will be taken away. That means if you break the rules, you might not get to see Rocky for a while. Do you understand?" she asked.

"Can I see Rocky now?" Robert pleaded.

"Sure. You can only stay for a little while today, it will soon be time for dinner; we all must to eat at the same time. I'll come and tell you when you're to come inside."

The sanatorium campus was fairly large with a retaining fence around the perimeter. A smaller fenced area was provided for the various animals. Pinky took Robert to Rocky, when he saw Robert he began to run and bark enthusiastically. When the gate was opened he ran and jumped on Robert, licking his hands and face, then ran a few feet away, turned and looked at Robert, then with one bark, ran and reared up on him. Robert sat down and leaned back against the fence and talked to Rocky, "Rocky, we got a new home now, I reckon we can't sit by the tree and listen to the water and watch the other animals. Maybe the people won't laugh at me or be mean to you. Maybe someday we will see Pepe again. Pepe is the only friend I have in the whole world, just you and Pepe."

Rocky, with his head slightly tilted, listened intently as Robert talked and nestled closer to him.

Much too soon Pinky came and told Robert it was time for dinner.

"Can I bring Rocky with me?" Robert asked.

"No, you may not bring Rocky with you!! You know the rules!" she declared sharply.

"I don't want to eat," Robert said, "I want to stay with Rocky."

"Robert! Don't be difficult, if you don't do as you are told, you'll be confined to quarters, then you won't be able to see Rocky at all."

"I don't know 'confined to quarters'" he said

"It means you can't go outside at all," she said.

In a voice much like the roaring of a lion, Robert yelled, "NO! I don't want to stay in the house!" and began to run toward the fence.

Pinky blew her whistle, signaling trouble; soon two huge men came to take control of Robert. They took him to what they referred to as 'security', which consisted of a bed and a chamber pot; locked the door from the outside and left him.

For a very long time he continued to cry out in his booming voice: "I don't want to be here; I want to be with my friends Rocky and Pepe; I want to go to my tree by the stream"

Finally his voice lowered to a moan and he eventually fell asleep.

Morning came, Pinky, along with two security people came to Robert's room, knocked on the door and waited a couple of minutes then opened the door.

"Good morning Robert," Pinky said, "are you hungry?"

Slowly Robert, who was sitting with is back to the door, turned to look at the people standing at the door. For the longest time he just stared at them, then, in a subdued voice,

"Can I go home now, I don't want to be here anymore."

"I'm sorry Robert, you can't go home now," Pinky said.

Becoming more and more agitated, Robert began to wail in his loud-booming voice, "Why does everyone hate me?"

"We don't hate you, Robert," Pinky said.

"People laugh at me, no one wants to be my friend—only Pepe. Can Pepe come to see me."

Gently placing her hand on Robert's shoulder, "I'm sure he can, if you will stop crying and come to breakfast, I'll see if Pepe can come see you.," Pinky assured him.

Robert continued to sit without talking.

After a long pause, Pinky said, "Robert."

Still he remained silent.

Finally, "Robert, are you coming to breakfast? If you don't come now, you can't have anything to eat until lunch time," Pinky said sternly.

After another long pause she continued, "Because you won't cooperate, you won't be allowed to see Rocky today."

"If I eat breakfast can I see Rocky?" he asked.

"If you will cooperate, you may spend time with Rocky,"

On the way to the kitchen Robert asked, "Can you tell Pepe to come to see me?"

"I don't know Pepe or how to find him. Do you know his address?" Pinky asked.

"His mother likes him, so he stays with her," Robert said. "My mother doesn't like me, I think she made me come here."

"Does your mother know Pepe?"

As he dropped his head, in the saddest tone of voice, said," I don't know if she likes him. I may never see Pepe again," and began to cry silently.

"I'll try to find him and ask him to come see you."

After he hurriedly ate his breakfast, Robert said, "Can I see Rocky now?"

Again Rocky was ecstatic when Robert approached the kennel.

After a long talk with Rocky, Robert's spirits began to be lifted.

CHAPTER 7

The Visit

After searching the records, Pinky found the address of Robert's mother and sent a request for information about Pepe.

The letter came and contained this message:

I want nothing to do with that beast, but I've included the person's address where his friend Pepe stays. Myrtle.

Pinky could hardly believe her eyes; the thought came, *"Look who's calling someone a beast!" How could a mother develop such an attitude as that. Robert is one lucky guy by coming here.*

Robert was non-communicative and stayed to himself, mostly in the day room when he wasn't out with Rocky. He would doodle a while, color a while, then wad the paper and throw it in the trash. No one gave a thought as to what he was throwing away.

"Did you learn to read and write while you were in school?" Pinky asked Robert.

"Yes a little, I can spell dog; rocky is a dog. I can spell Momma, but she doesn't like me so I don't spell her," he answered, tears came to his eyes, "I wish I was good like other people so Momma would like me."

Pinky patted his shoulder, tears welling up in her eyes, "Robert you are as good as anyone on the earth, just because your Momma doesn't want you, doesn't mean other people don't like you. I like you very much and you and I are going to become very good friends. When you feel lonely or when you want someone to talk to, I want you to come find me, I want to talk to you anytime." Pinky gently pulled him close to her and hugged him. He did not hug back.

After learning Pepe's address, Pinky quickly found Robert and gave him the news,

"We have Pepe's address now so you can write him a letter and ask him to come see you," Pinky said gleefully.

Pinky sent Pepe's folks a letter explaining the situation with Robert and asked if it be possible for Pepe to visit Robert.

An answer came very soon, asking for visiting procedure and would one day be better than another?

Pinky wrote that any day, at their convenience, would be fine, but a prior notice of the visit would be appreciated.

At last the day came! Pinky had not told Robert of Pepe's coming, wanting it to be a surprise. Robert had been reclusive for days, the only time he showed interest in anything was when he played with Rocky.

He finished his breakfast and was at the table in the day room doodling. He looked up and saw Pepe, jumped to his feet, threw pencil, colors, and paper everywhere, then roared, "Pepe!" and ran to him, "Pepe! Pepe! Hey Pinky, this is my friend Pepe. Pepe thinks I'm good like other people, Pepe, Rocky and me—we're all friends.

Miss Pinky, can Pepe and me play with Rocky now?"

"Yes you may, I'll take you there," she said.

Once outside and to Rocky's pen, as usual, he was bouncing around all over, anxious for the gate to be opened. He ran first to Robert, and then as though he remembered Pepe, ran to him. The three of them romped 'til they were exhausted; Rocky, jumping on one and then the other. Sitting with their backs to the fence, Robert told of his and Rocky's trip to the mountain and getting lost.

"If it hadn't been for Rocky, I might still be up there. Rocky's smart, he knew how to get home."

Then he told Pepe about his Momma hurting Rocky and how he tried to get her to stop. "She made the sheriff bring me here; she said she was afraid of me."

"How long will you have to stay here?" Pepe asked.

"'Til I die I reckon," he answered, "it's not real bad. No one here laughs at me and they are good to Rocky. We can see each other everyday."

"Can you draw pictures here?" Pepe asked.

"Yeah, I think I can but I haven't yet, I don't see any critters in here except old dogs and cats; they ain't pretty like foxes and things that live on the mountain."

"That's alright Bobo; people like to see drawings even if the things you draw are ugly."

"I think my Momma is ugly—maybe I could show you what she looks like to me," Robert said.

With that he proceeded to the table where the pencils, colors, and paper stay. Shortly, Robert showed Pepe what he had drawn. An old skinny hag with a snarl on her lips, revealing only one tooth in front; eyes drawn down in such a way as to depict evil; her straggly, unkempt hair and a torn and ragged dress gave way to legs that resembled slightly enlarged tooth picks, disappearing into worn-out combat boots.

As he looked at it, Pepe actually gasped! "Is this how your Momma looks to you?"

"Yeah, she's ugly, that's how she looks to me," Robert answered.

"Bobo, can I have this picture?"

"Yeah—sure, you are my friend," he answered

"May I show it to my Momma, please" Pepe implored.

"Yeah, you can show it to your Momma but don't let my Momma see it."

"Since you're not gonna be around those mean kids at school, who might laugh at you, may I show my Momma the picture of the possum and the fox?" Pepe asked

After thinking a few moments, he said, "Yeah, I reckon that'll be alright,"

Finally, Pepe's Mom said it was time to go.

"Can Pepe come back again?" Robert asked.

"Yes, of course—we'll come back to see you . . ."

As Robert lay in bed, re-living the day, he drifted off to sleep. Suddenly he, Rocky, and Pepe were at the old tree at the school yard.

"Let's climb the mountain today Pepe!" Robert said enthusiastically.

"What a wonderful idea!" Pepe said.

Off they went up the side of the mountain, "Are your legs tired Pepe?

"No! I'm doing real good."

Soon they were in a cloud, hardly able to see each other but climbing faster and faster until eventually they burst out of the cloud, revealing the most beautiful sight either had ever seen.

"Do you need to stop and rest Pepe?" Robert asked.

"No! Let's go on to the top!" he replied.

At the top they could see other mountains and the huge valleys below. Being above the tree line, they could see the clouds below.

"I'm going to jump on that cloud we just came through! It looks so fluffy, it won't hurt when I land on it." Robert said, and before Pepe could register an objection, Robert was on his way. As he sailed right through the cloud, he returned to reality with a thud.

For several moments, he wondered if Pepe and Rocky were still up on that mountain.

CHAPTER 8

Pinky The Tutor

At the staff meeting, Pinky rose and said, "I know we aren't suppose to get involved in the personal lives of our patients but I'd like to have permission to try teaching Robert Harrell to read and write. He has no one who cares about him; no family and only one friend who has limited means of communicating with him. Even though he is somewhat retarded, I think there is something about him we're overlooking."

"You know there are dangers in this. While we might develop certain elements of his mind, there will be others that can't be developed," the director said. "He came to us with a reputation of violent behavior."

"Yes Sir, I'm aware of that," Pinky said, "but having observed him for some time now, I believe there is a possibility that his prior behavior just might be altogether something else. In his mind, he feels he did nothing wrong. His mother wants nothing to do with him; may I read a letter we received from her, [*I want nothing to do with that beast*]. Isn't it just possible she falsely used what was intended to be an act of kindness, to get him out of her life? Robert's reaction to her hurting his dog was, I think, an effort to protect the only thing in his life that really cared for him.

That fact alone seems to me to depict a characteristic of kindness and not of hostility."

"You have a noble ambition Pinky, but there are certain things to consider that are unique to people like Robert. Right now, he has nothing to attract him to anything outside this institution. It was determined at his hearing he was not capable of functioning in open society. To advance his education, just might increase his desire to leave and if that happened and he returned to his violent nature, would he be better off in a prison than here with us?" the director asked.

"We all agree than learning to read and write opens a whole new world to anyone, and in this case, it almost seems criminal not to teach Robert," Pinky argued.

"He has been declared a ward of the state and consequently, whatever he does, be it good or bad, we will be held responsible," the director insisted.

"I'm absolutely confident, he poses no liability to this institution, I can see no reason why we shouldn't give him this opportunity to improve his life," Pinky insisted.

"Do any of you on the board have anything to say in this matter?" The director asked.

Since no one spoke up, he turned to Pinky and said, "You seem to have given this a lot of thought, so until such time we might deem this unsatisfactory, you have permission to do what you can for the guy."

"Thank you, you'll never regret it," as she shook the hand of the director.

CHAPTER 9

Robert's Talent Revealed

"Mom when we get home, I want to show you something," Pepe said to his mother, after leaving the sanatorium.

"Sure son," she said, "what is it?"

"I don't want to tell you, I want to show you."

"Very well, we'll be home soon."

As they pulled into their driveway, Pepe eagerly ran to his room and from his secret place, retrieved the earlier drawing by Robert.

"Mom, before I show you these, you must promise me never to tell or show these to anyone. Do you promise?"

"Of course Pepe, what on earth do you have there?" she asked.

As she looked at the two papers: one of the possum and one of the fox. Slowly, she raised her eyes to meet Pepe's and with a quizzical look said, "Where did you get these?!"

"Bobo drew them," he said, then paused to see what his mother's reaction was going to be.

She said nothing, just looked at Pepe in a disbelieving way.

"You don't believe me do you?" he said

"Are you telling me Robert Harrell drew these pictures?" she asked.

"Yes, I watched him do it. Look at what he drew for me today," and handed his mother the picture Robert had drawn of his mother.

As she sat gazing at the hideous picture, tears filled her eyes as she took Pepe in her arms and held him to her breast for the longest time. Finally, she held him back at arm's length and asked, "Pepe, is this how your mother looks to you?"

"No Mom! You look beautiful to me." Again she pulled him to her and said, "I love you my son!"

"Mom, when Bobo drew these pictures he made me promise I would never show them to anyone; he was afraid people would laugh at him. Today, when he drew his mother I asked him for permission to show all of them to you, he said only, 'I guess it'll be alright' and I think he meant you were the only one to see them. Please, don't tell anyone about them Mom; please?"

"Of course I won't Bobo, but this boy has a remarkable talent and someone needs to know about it. Do you think he is capable of understanding that he has a special talent?"

"He draws only what he sees; the way he sees it. He doesn't want anyone to see what he draws 'cause he's afraid people will laugh at him," Pepe said.

"Well, let's give him a little more time at the institution and see what happens; for now, let's keep these things to ourselves," his mother said.

CHAPTER 10

Lessons

As was usual, Pinky came to get Robert for breakfast.

"Robert, today we're going to do something special. How would you like to learn to write? I mean more things than just mom; maybe we can learn to write Rocky; how would you like that?" Pinky asked.

"If I learn to write Rocky, will you laugh at me?" Robert asked.

"NO! NO! NO Robert, I will never laugh at you; I believe you can learn to write Rocky real good!"

"How do I learn?" he asked.

"I'll show you and you can do it just like me. First let's eat our breakfast."

Robert hurriedly ate his breakfast and turned to Pinky and asked, "Can I see Rocky now?"

"Yes you may, but let's start learning to write real soon."

At the table in the day room, Pinky arranged all the pencils and paper and sat down with Robert.

"First, I'll make a letter, then you make it just like mine," Pinky began and proceeded to make the R. When she gave Robert the pencil and watched him copy it, she could hardly believe her eyes; his R looked exactly like the one she'd made.

Noticing Pinky's reaction and thinking he had done badly Robert said, "I'm sorry Miss Pinky, that's what it looks like to me."

For a moment Pinky sat silently looking at Robert, finally said, "That's real good Robert, let's try an O."

After making the O she gave Robert the pencil, again the same results; Robert's O looked exactly like hers. "Robert, that's very good, let's see if you can make R o c k y."

Robert took the pencil and wrote ROCKY which looked exactly like Pinky's.

"Do you know what that spells," she asked.

"I don't know what is 'spells', he said.

Pointing to the word Pinky said, "That spells Rocky. That's how Rocky looks"

Robert became visibly upset and said "No! It don't look like Rocky!"

"I know it doesn't look like Rocky, but that's how you spell Rocky," Pinky said, now having some personal questions such as, *'What have I gotten myself into?*

"Now let's put all the letters in a row and we can learn what sound they make and soon you'll know what 'spell' means," and proceeded to write the alphabet.

"Now let's learn the name on each letter; the first three are: A B C. Say this after me,

"A B C" After she finished she looked at Robert. He sat silent for a moment then looked at Pinky, saying nothing. "Can you say ABC?" she asked. Again he sat staring at the letters. Finally he said, "ABC. I don't want to know 'spell'."

"That's a good start, Robert; you'll begin to have fun learning once we get into it. After a while you can write Pepe a letter and he can write you one and send it to you, then when he can't come to see you, you can write and tell him all about Rocky, doesn't that sound like fun? You can write him everyday and he can write you everyday. But first you have to learn to read. OK?" Pinky asked.

"If I write him a letter will someone else see it?" Robert asked, "Sometimes people laugh at me, it makes me feel real bad."

"Only the ones you want to read you letter will be able to," Pinky assured him. "No one here will ever laugh at you and I'm sure Pepe won't."

Robert's progress was slow but Pinky was very patient. Finally he began to understand what to do with the letters, although he was not able to say the A.B.C'S from A-Z, he did understand what they were for. Pinky wrote the letters from A-Z on a sheet and left them for Robert to refer to from time to time.

"How would you like to spell Pepe today, Robert," Pinky asked.

"Can I write him a letter today?," Robert asked.

"First we have to learn to spell some words. When we learn those we can write Pepe.

First let's learn to spell 'Pepe'." Pinky said, "I'll write Pepe and you look at the sheet with the letters on it and pick out the letters that spell Pepe."

This she did and to her amazement, Robert very quickly picked out the letters.

"Now Robert can you look at the sheet and write the letters that spell Pepe?" she asked.

He picked the correct letters but didn't arrange them to spell Pepe.

"You see Robert they have to be in line just as I have written them. Again she wrote the word Pepe. Now write them just as I have."

Robert took the pencil and wrote *Pepe* that looked the very same as Pinky's.

Again Pinky was astonished at the similarity.

"Miss Pinky, will you be my friend?" Robert asked.

Pinky was taken aback by the abrupt question. "Of course I'll be your friend," she said

"I only have one friend besides Rocky, I'm glad you'll be my friend," Robert said.

With a grave sense of pity, Pinky asked, "Robert, would you mind if I hug you?"

"I don't know, I liked it when you hugged me before." he said.

Pinky took Robert into her arms and hugged him snugly; Robert simply stood with his arms at his sides.

"I like being hugged Miss Pinky," he said.

Somewhat shaken by the realization of the inner torment this pitiful lad must have endured, "That's all we'll do today; you may go play with Rocky now if you'd like."

Pinky went to her room and cried for awhile, more determined than ever to bring this boy into the real world.

CHAPTER 11

The Revelation

Robert's progress was slow but steady. He could now put together letters to make small words: cat, dog, cow, etc. Pinky would, at times, question her own devotion to the task, but considering the situation fully, would ultimately find the will to continue.

As they sat chatting, Pinky asked, "Robert do you ever think of your mother?"

"My Momma don't like me so I don't think of her."

"Can you tell me what your mother looks like?" Pinky asked.

"I can show you what she looks like to me," taking the pencil and a sheet of paper he began to draw, soon handed Pinky the picture of the emaciated old hag he had drawn for Pepe. Stunned, Pinky could say nothing, first by the quality of the drawing and secondly of his perception of his mother.

"How did you learn to draw like that?" Pinky asked.

"That's how she looks to me," he said.

"Can you draw other things?" she asked.

"I just draw things like they look to me," he answered.

"Can you draw Rocky?" she asked

Robert began to draw and soon handed Pinky the paper.

Again Pinky was amazed as she sat staring at the picture of Rocky, sitting, his ears perked slightly upward, his mouth open that looked for the world like a smile.

"May I keep these pictures?" Pinky asked.

"You're my friend and you can have them but don't show them to anyone else; they might laugh at me; I don't like for people to laugh at me."

"May I show them to someone if I promise they will not laugh at you?" Pinky asked.

"If you're sure they won't laugh, you may."

"Would you like to go play with Rocky now?" she asked.

"REALLY!! Can I go see him now?" he asked.

Pinky rose to her feet and pulled Robert to her in a big hug.

"I like for you to hug me, I feel so safe when you do," Robert said, and off to see Rocky.

With the drawings in hand, Pinky headed to the directors office.

"Are you finally giving up on Robert?" the director asked.

Laying the drawings on his desk, she asked, "What do you think?"

"What's this?" he asked.

"Believe it or not, Robert drew these two pictures in less than 5 minutes."

"Are you kidding me," he asked and not waiting for her answer, let out a long and loud whistle. Continuing to examine the drawings he asked, "Did he have something to look at, some pattern to go by while he was drawing?!"

"Nothing! I ask if he missed his mother and he said his mother didn't like him so he didn't think of her. I ask if she was pretty and he simply said, 'I'll show you how she looks to me' and drew that sketch of her."

"I've heard of such gifted people but have never actually met one. You'd not expect a person like Robert to have such a gift," the director said.

"What are we to do with these developments?" Pinky asked. "We shouldn't just overlook his potential; we have the moral obligation to help him capitalize on it. It's certain he has no idea of what he has."

The director, silent for a moment, then added, "If and when the mother learns of these circumstances, she will try to re-claim custody of Robert and I'm not sure we can prevent that."

"I'm absolutely convinced Robert doesn't want to go back to her," Pinky said.

"Here's what I think we ought to do. Give this a few more days, keep teaching him the things you've been teaching. We'll suggest he do some art work along; that'll give us a better idea of what his capabilities and limitations are. At some point, we'll have to bring some expert into the matter; by then we'll know better how to proceed."

As the lessons continued, Pinky would occasionally ask Robert to draw something; each time the drawings were absolutely perfect.

"Robert, do you think you could draw me? Pinky asked.

"I can draw you like you look to me," he said and began to draw.

Soon he handed Pinky the drawing; an angel with beautiful white wings in a flowing white gown, suspended above the earth, a halo above her head.

"This is how you look to me," he said.

Shaken, and at a loss for words, Pinky simply stared at the drawing for the longest time.

Finally she took Robert by the hand and pulled him to her in a big hug. "Robert, that's the nicest thing anyone ever did for me, you're amazing."

"Since my Momma don't like me, would you be my Momma," he asked.

She couldn't answer; she just pulled him closer to her.

CHAPTER 12

Robert Learns To Write

Finally, with Pinky's help, Robert learned enough words to write Pepe a letter:

Dear Pepe, you come see me, I can write now. Robert.

Pepe anxiously tore open the envelope and read the words.

"I got a letter from Bobo, he wants me to come see him again; can we Momma?"

"Yes, we'll go see him. We'll have to go Saturday so you want miss school," she said, "You don't want to miss school."

"Pepe I know I promised not to show Bobo's drawings to anyone," his mother began, "and I won't if you are sure I shouldn't. Robert has a talent unlike anyone I've seen. I believe if the right people see his work, it could mean a lot of things: money, recognition, honor and I think it would do a lot for his esteem. You know he is very sensitive, always feeling that no one cares about him and people poke fun at him. If we talk to the people at the sanatorium, they could do many good things for your friend."

"I'm sure Bobo wants people to like him, but he feels so badly when people laugh at him, he's afraid to show his drawings." Bobo said, "We could take our drawing and talk to him about the possibilities; maybe he would give us permission to go ahead."

Saturday came and they made the trip to the sanatorium. Again, Robert was overjoyed at the sight of his friend; anxious to tell about Pinky teaching him to write and having more time to spend with Rocky. Then on to the kennel where Rocky was every bit as happy to see Pepe as he was Robert.

After frolicking until they were exhausted, they sat down with their backs to the kennel, Rocky nestled close to Robert, wanting to be rubbed and petted. Pepe and Robert reliving the times they spent at the old tree and stream, Robert re-asserting his deep desire to climb the mountain and see the other side.

Finally Pepe began, "Bobo, I know I promised not to show your drawings to anyone except my Momma, but she thinks you have a talent which could mean a lot of money for you if you would let other people see them. People wouldn't laugh at you; we think they would pay you money to draw for them."

"Miss Pinky asked me to draw Momma, and then she asked me to draw her. I think she liked them," Robert said.

"You let Miss Pinky see your drawings?" he asked.

"Yes."

"Did Miss Pinky laugh?"

"No, I think she liked them," Robert said.

"I think people would give you money for pictures like you draw," Pepe said, "would you like that?"

"I Think I would—why would people give me money for pictures?" Robert asked.

Pepe, trying hard to help Bobo understand, said, "It's called *ART*! They put your pictures in frames and hang them on their walls. When people come to their house they ask who drew the picture and that way they find out it's you, then those people come to you and have you draw for them, then they give you money."

Finally it was time for Pepe and his Mom to leave for home.

"Pepe, you write me a letter; Miss Pinky will tell you how. Someday me and you will climb that old mountain."

"I promise; I'll write you a letter." Pepe said as they were leaving.

CHAPTER 13

Old Clyde And Kitty

There were those living in the sanatorium because they had no other place to live; not because of some wrongful thing they'd done. Many of these people had come to know Robert and of his talent. They were often the subjects of his drawing. In addition, there were relatives who came to visit. Robert soon became the center of attraction at the sanatorium. Among those who came regularly was a very pretty young lady named Kitty.

Kitty came to visit her Grandpa, known only as 'Old Clyde'. Clyde was a grouchy old coot but was liked by all. When chided about being grouchy, he'd say, "When you've lived as long as I have, you've earned the right to be grouchy."

Robert always looked forward to seeing Kitty but was reluctant to speak to her privately. She always wanted to see what new things he had drawn.

One day as she was examining his new drawings, she asked. "Robert, would you draw me?"

"Sure!" He then began to draw and soon handed her the drawing.

"OH MY! Robert, that is so good. May I have it for my own; I'll pay you for it." she exclaimed; "I'll keep it forever."

"I don't want you to pay me for it, I want to give it to you 'cause you're so pretty." Robert said, still uncertain.

"OH thank you!" she said and ran to Robert to gave him a big hug.

"You're welcome." he said, thinking how pretty she smelled and wanted to hug her back but decided against it.

"Let's sit and talk, I'd like to know about you. The people are so fond of you here and you have such a good-looking smile." She winked and smiled, took him by the hand and they walked to the table in the day room and sat down.

"I'm curious as to why you're here." Kitty began, "Did you do something you shouldn't have?"

Robert began to tell of his early life: how the kids his age laughed at him; how his mother loathed him; how he felt alone in the world. As the events of his life poured out, occasionally Kitty's eyes would fill with tears but she didn't interrupt.

He told her of his yearning to climb the big mountain and someday ride on one of those fluffy clouds. "I felt like Pepe and Rocky were the only friends I had in the world."

Robert grew silent. The two of them sat for several moments. Robert, just staring down at his hands, suddenly realized he had been wringing them as he told his story.

Kitty wanted to comfort him but couldn't decide how.

Finally, "Well, now you have lots of friends;" Kitty said, "friends who like you and admire you. Robert, I want you to know, I'm one of those friends."

Still too shy to be forward Robert said, "Knowing that you are my friend makes me very happy."

CHAPTER 14

Rocky's Demise

Even with all the association with the people around him, Robert always found time to spend with his friend Rocky. The two of them seemed to make each other happy. Robert would sit for long periods of time talking to Rocky as though he was speaking to another person. Rocky would respond by wagging his tail and sometimes jump up and run a circle, come back in front of Robert and lower his head between his front feet as though he were stretching then bound toward Robert. Eventually it became obvious, Rocky wasn't the energetic animal he once was. Robert could tell he was getting old but refused to accept it. He would ask the veterinarian to see about him. For a while, the medicine would make Rocky feel better, but it soon became obvious Rocky was declining. He was no longer able to frolic when Robert went to be with him; instead the only thing he was still able to move with vigor was his tail.

Inevitably, the day came when the vet told Robert, "Son, there's nothing more we can do for Rocky. We now have only two options: we can do nothing and he'll be in severe pain for a few days and finally pass away or we can give him a shot and he will simply go to sleep, feeling no more pain."

Stunned, Robert said, "I don't want him to die, but I don't want him to be in pain. Can I hold him while he goes to sleep?"

"Of course."

"Can I have a little while to talk to him before he goes sleep?" Robert asked.

"Take as long as you like," the vet said.

Robert picked up Rocky and carried him outside the pen, "You shouldn't have to die in prison," he said. They sat down outside the pen and Robert began to talk.

"Rocky, in a way, you and I are alike. We were once in this world without a friend or a place where we could feel safe. It was a very special day when you came to me at the old school; I needed a friend and you needed a friend. I truly hope you found happiness in our friendship; I certainly did."

Rocky looked up at Robert with sad eyes, as though he understood and agreed.

"They tell me it's time for you to go to sleep forever; someday it will be my time to go to sleep forever. I hope we can find each other in the next life; then we can climb that old mountain and this time, finally get to the top.

Rocky had been laying with his head on Robert's lap. Suddenly, he lifted his head, made a long whining sound, then laid his head back on Robert's lap and simply stopped breathing.

Robert pulled him to his chest and began to cry loudly. The vet and the director, who had been waiting a short distance away, hastily made their way to Robert to offer comfort.

Without saying anything the vet put his hand on Robert's shoulder.

"Thank you," Robert said, "I'm sorry, it's just that he meant so much to me. I'll be alright."

Robert obtained permission to take Rocky outside the compound and bury him. When finished, he sought Pinky and began to tell about Rocky. Pinky interrupted him and told him she had seen the whole thing.

Again tears began to fill Robert's eyes, "Miss Pinky, will you hug me?"

She hastily pulled him to her and this time Robert hugged her back; she was surprised at his strength.

"I'm so sorry Robert. I know how fond you were of him."

"Miss Pinky, will you help me send Pepe a letter to tell him about Rocky?"

"Of course; but you shouldn't need much help; let's go do that right now." she said.

Pepe, Rocky died. You come see where I bury him. Pepe, I cried, I couldn't help it.

CHAPTER 15

Going Public

As the months turned into years, the old school consolidated with the city school, leaving the building to the elements. It's now referred to as *'the old schoolhouse at the foot of the mountain'*.

Robert's progress was remarkable; it was almost like a door had been opened into his mind. He was capable of interacting with grow-ups on their level; he came to understand his ability to draw as something special and was willing to follow the requests of people who asked for his service.

Pinky kept all the drawings and had them filed away. At the board meeting, Pinky brought the subject up.

"I think we should give some consideration to marketing Robert's work. Two things are obvious:

1. He has a marketable talent and it seems to me, since he is a ward of the state, it becomes our responsibility for preparing him for his life after he becomes eligible for release from us.

2. It is my considered opinion, his potential for competing in the work-force, outside his talent, is not very promising."

After pausing briefly, she added, "If we are to help him in this way, special rules and regulations may have to be added to our charter."

Turning to the other 8 board members the director said, "Let's hear some ideas."

"It seems to me to be either unethical, immoral, or illegal, if not all three, to force, by law, this lad into this institution and then profit from his abilities." One of them said.

"It's obvious he has to have a lot of help in getting his work to the public, and since Pinky has brought him this far, she should be allowed a percentage of the revenue to obtain supplies, displays, and marketing techniques. and/or other expenses which may be incurred in the course of these duties," another member added.

Still another asked, "What about his mother? Will she be able to take part in this thing?"

"Of course we'll have to look into that but since she relinquished her interest in him; and we have her letter stating that she wanted nothing to do with him, referring to him as a beast, I don't foresee a problem with her." the director said.

Pinky rose to speak, "As most of you know, the boy is very dear to me. I'll be happy to assume responsibility for his entrance into the business world; as a matter of fact, if none of you have an objection, I'd like to be his first customer. Robert drew me as an angel. Now you all know I'm no angel, but because no one had ever shown an interest in him before, maybe that's the way he saw me, I certainly hope so.

'I don't know much about the value of art, so I'm offering $50.00 for his drawing. If there are those of you who think that's not enough, I'll pay whatever is fair. Also, we all should agree on a fair percentage I should receive for managing his affairs; I think 15% of sales is fair; that should be sufficient for materials, for which I will pay.

"Let's hear other comments," the director said.

"I've never seen a talent as pure as this lad possesses, there doesn't seem to be a flaw in it," one of the members said. "Like Pinky, I don't know the value of his work, maybe we should set up a display here in the day room and offer for sale some of his drawings; I'm sure visitors will be interested; some might even want him to do a portrait for themselves."

"So far, we've only seen his work on **8 ½ x 11**, we should see if his work is as good on an enlarged background," another offered.

"That's a great idea!" Pinky said, "Let's ask him to do his dog Rocky on a **16x16**."

"Do we know if his talent extends to painting; if not, could we teach him?" the director asked.

"We can ask him to do something with paints and see how it goes." Pinky said, "First, let's have him do the dog on a larger background."

Pinky went to the day room where Robert spent most of his time since Rocky died.

"Robert, could I talk to you please?"

"Have I done something wrong, Miss Pinky?" he asked.

"Oh no, nothing like that; I want to talk about your drawings. We believe we can sell them for money. What we would like for you to do, is draw Rocky on bigger paper. Would you do that?" she asked.

"What do you mean—on bigger paper?" Robert asked.

"You know, make the picture of Rocky bigger. Can you do that?"

"If you have some bigger paper, I'll draw Rocky; I like to draw Rocky, he was a good friend." Robert said, the sadness in his eyes was obvious.

Pinky soon returned with poster board and cut him a piece 16x16. "Make Rocky big." Pinky said. "I'll be back shortly to see how you are doing. If you have questions, just ask."

Shortly Robert brought Pinky his drawing and it was, as expected, a masterpiece. Rocky was sitting, his ears perked up with what looked like a big smile on his mouth.

"Robert you're fantastic! I'll get you a frame and you can put it in your room and rocky can always be close to you." After poring over the drawing for several moments, reluctantly, added, "Robert how would you like to have your pictures where everyone who comes here could admire them. We think they would want to buy them and give you money. Maybe some might want you to draw a picture of themselves."

"Would they laugh at my pictures?" he asked.

"NO!NO! They will be very happy to see how you can draw.'

"If they won't laugh at me, I'll do it." he said.

The director took the picture from Pinky and after some time, slowly turn his head from the picture and said, "This is truly unbelievable!"

"I have spoken to Robert about setting up a display and offering his drawings for sale and he has agreed. I think we should have them in frames and if that's agreeable, I'll spend the fifty dollars I've paid for my picture to obtain the frames and other materials for the display.

"There's no better time than right now to kick this thing off. Maybe some of the maintenance men could build us a back drop for the display, you can do the shopping for supplies; if you need anything, just let me know." he said.

Hesitating, Pinky asked, "What do you think about asking Robert to draw 'Old Clyde'?"

Chuckling, the director said, "Sounds like a wonderful idea; that might even make him smile."

"I reckon we should ask Old Clyde for permission first; I'll do that now." Pinky offered.

Gathering up several of Robert's drawings, Pinky made her way to Old Clyde's room. A couple of raps on the door, Clyde asked, in his grouchiest tone, "Who is it?!"

"It's me, Pinky; I have something to show you."

"What if I don't want to see what you have to show me," he continued.

"AW! Come on Clyde, you know you like me, and I would never show you something you didn't want to see."

"The door ain't locked; it ain't never locked; nobody can have any privacy around here."

"You're just a pussycat trying to act like a tiger. You know we love you and you make us happy just by being Clyde," Pinky said, certain she detected a faint smile from Old Clyde.

"Well? What is it you want to show me?"

"I want you to look at some of the drawings by the young man we call Robert. They are very good. If you'll permit us, we'd like to have him draw your picture and use it in the center of a display we're setting up for him. We think there's a market for his drawings and if that's true, we can help him establish his work and eventually be able to make it on his own." she explained.

"Is that the kid that hangs around my Kitty?" Clyde asked.

"Yes, he seems to be quite fond of Kitty." Pinky said.

"Ain't he retarded? How can he know how to draw anything?"

"Maybe I can't explain, but his talent comes from God. Frankly," she said, "I've never seen anything like it. Did Kitty show you the picture he drew of her?"

"Yes." Clyde said with no emotion whatsoever.

Both grew quiet. Pinky was about to abandon the idea when Clyde opened up, "Well I reckon it'll be aright for him to do his thing, but if I don't like it, you can't put it on no display."

"That's fair enough." Pinky said, adding. "Clyde, I have to warn you, this lad, before coming here, didn't know what love was. His school mates laughed and made fun of him; his mother mistreated him from the time he was born; she hated him and called him a beast. I'm convinced she lied in order to get him committed to this facility. Even though he's been here all these months, he still hasn't learned to trust. His greatest fear is that someone will laugh and make fun of his work."

When and where does he want to do this thing?" Clyde asked.

"I'm sure he can do it anytime. When will be a good time for you?" she asked

"Well, I'll check my calender to see when I have an opening. Otherwise, if you don't hear from me, he can do it at his convenience," Clyde said snidely.

"Robert, you know how we made Rocky bigger on the paper?" Pinky asked.

"Yes, was it alright to make him bigger?"

"Yes, of course, he's so much prettier. Would you draw 'Old Clyde' for me? I want to put him in the middle of our display."

"Old Clyde will laugh at me." Robert said.

"NO! He won't; I promise, he wants you to draw him. Could you draw him bigger? Bigger even than Rocky?" Pinky asked, becoming more excited as things began to develop.

"I can draw him as big as the paper if you want me to." He said.

With the 24"x 30" poster on the easel and Old Clyde in place, Robert began to make marks. As far as Clyde could tell, it certainly didn't look like him!

Robert seldom looked at Old Clyde, but continued to make marks. Soon Clyde began to recognize certain things, then shapes began to develop; Clyde sat astounded and speechless.

In 30 minutes or less, from beginning to completion, Pinky, the director and Clyde marveled at what stood before them; the drawing was prefect!

"I'll give $250.00 for this drawing after you're finished with whatever you're going to do with it," Clyde said.

Pinky's head swam and for a minute she thought she'd pass out, "Well thank you Clyde, and you can certainly have it when we're finished."

"When Kitty comes again, I have her to get you the money."

The maintenance men built a wrap around backdrop, in the corner of the day room. Pinky bought frames for 30 of Robert's drawing: some of various wild animals; some of the people at the sanatorium and of course one of Rocky. Perhaps, next to Rocky's was Robert's favorite; it was one of Pepe with his twisted legs, smiling broadly with his hand extended as if to anticipate a hand shake.

CHAPTER 16

Pepe Visits

Pepe opened his letter from Robert, his Mom watched as tears filled his eyes; "What's wrong Pepe?" she asked

For several moments, Pepe was unable to answer.

"Has something happened to Bobo?" she insisted.

Finally, he slowly looked up at his Mom and said, "Rocky's dead Mom—Rocky's dead. Bobo wants me to come see where he buried him. Can we go Mom?? Can we?"

"Sure we'll go very soon. It'll be be a few weeks before I can manage it; but we will go as soon as possible."

Everyday, Pepe would remind his mom of the impending day when they could go see Robert and where he buried Rocky.

Finally the day came, Pepe's Mom said, "Pepe, we can go see Robert Saturday if you want to." Pepe let out a YAHOO!!

Again, they purposely didn't let Robert know they were coming so as to surprise him. When Robert saw Pepe come in he too let out a roar which sounded much like a lion.

"Pepe! My friend Pepe," then ran to give him a big hug.

Immediately, Robert took Pepe's hand and said, "Come let me show you where I buried Rocky." The two went rushing out to the back.

Pinky welcomed Pepe's Mom and invited her to see the display of drawings.

In a disbelieving tone she asked, "Are you telling me the boy has drawn these pictures?"

"Yes, that's what I'm telling you, and furthermore there are many more waiting for room to display them. We intend to offer these for sale as a means of preparing Robert for a life on his own."

Overcoming her astonishment, Pepe's Mom said, "Robert gave Pepe three pictures: one of a possum, one of a fox and one of his mother. The one of his mother is a hideous thing and I believe that's the way she looks to him. I'd like to help with this if I may—may I give you $75.00 and keep the pictures we have?"

"Yes of course and thank you so much for your help. This boy has had a rough time up to now but he's finally learning how it feels to be loved and how to trust other people. I think it's harder for him to trust than to accept love."

"Would it be possible for him to come spend a weekend with Pepe sometime?"

Pinky didn't respond right away, finally said, "There's coming a time when he will be allowed to do that, but it may not be the right time just yet. He often speaks of the old school house, the big old tree, the little stream, the huge mountain and his plan sometime to climb it. You have to consider that for the first 8-10 years of his life, the only solace he found was at that place. He's now learning to broaden his view of the world around him and to trust people." Pausing long enough to see if Pepe's mom understood, continued,

"Robert is learning to read a little and to write a few simple words. He seems to be able to draw what he sees. He can write a word very well if he sees it, but to tell him to spell something, maybe dog, or cat, or some simple word, he still has difficulty with it."

"Pinky, I'm so thankful for your interest in 'Bobo', as Pepe calls him. He is not the person some have perceived him to be. Pepe is so fond of him and I know his judge of character."

"We came to realize that fact a long time ago." Pinky said.

The two grew silent, satisfied just to admire the display.

As the boys approached the burial sight, Robert began, "I buried Rocky out here, I didn't want him to be in jail. He got sick and couldn't run like he used to and the dog doctor said he hurt a lot and would die pretty soon, but, if I wanted him to, he could give him a shot and he would just go to sleep forever. Pepe, I didn't know what to do; I didn't want him to go to sleep forever, but I didn't want him to be hurting. I asked the doctor if I could hold him for a while and he said yes. I was holding him, talking to him and explaining going to sleep forever; and Pepe, he raised up his head from my lap and whined, then just laid his head down and stopped breathing. I think he was telling me goodbye. Pepe, I was so sad, I cried and cried; I couldn't help it."

"I cried too when I got your letter saying Rocky had died." Pepe added.

"Bobo, they don't have school at the old place. There ain't nothing there now, just the old schoolhouse and fence;

we go to town school now. There are lots more people go there than went to the old school. Now they make us go to school whether we want to or not."

"Do they still laugh at you for the way you walk and talk?" Robert asked.

"No, the teacher tells us we shouldn't treat other people mean; mostly, they don't say bad things now.

A wistful look came over Robert's face, "Is old Gordy in your new school?"

"Yeah, but he ain't mean no more, he helps me sometimes. I bet he wouldn't be mean to you either."

"Is old George Fincher still principal at the new school?" Robert asked.

"No, he got sent to another school," Pepe said, "we got a different one; he's not mean like old George was."

The two grew silent, their thoughts going back to those awful days when life was so miserable.

"Bobo, I'll be graduating from school soon. I'd like for you to come to see me graduate; would you do that?" Pepe asked.

"I'd really like to do that but I don't know how I could get there."

"Maybe Miss Pinky could bring you," suggested Pepe.

"I'll ask her, maybe she can bring me."

Pepe's Mom came to say it was time for them to leave. Reluctantly, Robert offered his hand and the two shook hands and said goodbye.

Pepe excitedly said, "Bobo is going to ask Miss Pinky to bring him to my graduation. Momma, do you think she will?"

"OH! I'm sure she will, if it's possible," she said.

CHAPTER 17

Birthday

"Do you know what we've overlooked since you've been here?" Pinky asked Robert.

Robert, with a quizzical look, said, "No, is it something I've done wrong?"

"No, of course not, you always think it's something you've done wrong. If a wrong has been done, it's that we've not given you a birthday party.'

"When is my birthday?" Robert asked.

"Do you not know when your birthday is?"

"No." he answered.

"Do you know how old you are?" Pinky asked.

"No; no one told me." he answered.

"You were born August 29th 1929. It's now past August, 1945. Now can you tell me how old you are?" Pinky asked.

"I don't know how," he answered.

"Remember how we learned arithmetic; how we had 5 marbles and took away 3 and we had 2 left? You learn how old you are by taking 1945 marbles, that's this year; and take away 1929 marbles, that's the year you were born and that leaves 16. So you are 16 years old now." Pinky said. She realized what she had described had confused him, yet she believed eventually Robert would understand.

"Let's finish the display, put Old Clyde in the middle, then give our adventure a name," Pinky said, to no one in particular.

"Do you think Kitty would come to my birthday party?" Robert asked Pinky.

"Well I bet you couldn't keep her from coming even if you wanted to." Pinky replied.

"Kitty said she liked me and she smells so pretty! I'd sure like for her to come," he replied.

"We'll set the date for your party and call her; would you like for us to get you presents?"

"You know what I'd like?" he asked. "I'd like a marker for Rocky's grave with his name on it."

"That's a great idea. We'll certainly get that for you. Let's set the date for one week from Saturday; that'll give us time to finish the display, to notify Pepe, maybe he can come to your party." Pinky said, becoming more and more excited as the plan unfolded.

"Do you have an idea for a name for your display?" Pinky asked Robert.

"No," he said.

"Since you love Pepe so much, and since he can never say your name just right: and since he has called you Bobo, how about we write:

DRAWINGSBYBOBO
I'll draw your choice while you watch

Then you can write *"by BOBO"*, people like for their drawing to be signed by the artist."

Robert showed little concern.

"What we have to do is have you draw a portrait of yourself to be displayed above the drawings. Can you draw yourself," Pinky asked.

"I don't know how I look to me," he answered.

"We can get you a big mirror and you can draw while sitting in front of it," Pinky suggested," Pinky said, "that way you can see how you look."

The big mirror was brought in and Robert began to draw. Pinky went about her business so as not to disturb him while he worked. It an incredible short period of time, Robert came to her and held the drawing.

Pinky could hardly believe her eyes, the drawing showed Robert sitting at the easel, even his sadness, which was ever present, was captured.

"Robert, that's fantastic! It's nothing short of amazing."

The picture was framed and eventually placed in the display above his other work.

Even before the display was completed, people began to buy the pictures. At first they charged $25.00 for the smaller ones and $45.00 for the larger ones without frames. Soon they realized the pictures were worth more and Robert would not be able to supply the demand, so they marked them up: $45.00 for the smaller ones and $60.00 for the larger ones, $85.00 for one the size of Old Clyde. Within a week, people thronged to see the display: some came to buy, some brought their pets to be drawn, some brought family pictures, some wanted their own picture, some came just to watch Robert draw. All were fascinated by his talent. In only one week, they had grossed more than $1000.00. Day after day people came in great numbers, the demand was so great, Robert was unable to complete some orders and forced to schedule them another day.

The day of the party, Robert was up early, anxious to learn if Kitty and Pepe would be there. He and Pinky neatly arranged the display. Old Clyde rolled out to the day room, stared at the display for a while, then finally turned to Pinky and shook his head,

"How did I live this long before seeing something like this?" he asked.

Pinky shrugged and said, "When I look at what this lad can do, I simply can't believe it." Adding, "Will Kitty be coming to the party?"

"Yeah, I reckon she will, that's all she talks about." Clyde said snidely.

Pinky discreetly glanced at Robert to see his happy, smiling face.

Pepe arrived before Kitty. When he saw the display cried "WOW! That's wonderful! I have an idea Bobo, lets put up a display at my graduation and then everyone will know about you! Wouldn't that be good?"

"OH NO! They would laugh at the drawings."

"No! I'm sure they wouldn't, you're all grown up now and besides, no one could laugh at these drawings; they are fantastic!"

Pinky standing nearby, over-heard the conversation, said, "What a wonderful idea! There will be many there who will want to buy your pictures; the school people will want to acknowledge and honor you. They will take great pride in the fact that you were a student at that school."

"I don't want my Momma to see my pictures.," Robert said.

Pinky, taking Robert by the hands and they sat down at the table, "Robert, I can't imagine the bitter feeling you must have for your mom and some of the children who went to school there when you did; I know it must be terrifying to think of seeing them again. Please, look at me, those things were long ago; they should not stay with you any more. You know how good it feels for me to hug you? That's the way most people feel when others show their love for them." Hesitating for a moment to see how Robert was processing what was said, she continued, "Young children, when they start to school want to be accepted. Some people feel important just by making sport of others; others who might never make sport of someone, want to be accepted by those that do; supposing they might be important simply by belonging."

Robert sat silent and motionless. "Do you understand?" Pinky asked.

"No, I don't understand why people want to hurt someone else; I don't understand why they want to laugh at others; I hurts real bad when people laugh at you."

Pinky, not knowing exactly how to continue, "Robert, you know I have never lied to you. I promise, no one will laugh at you when they see your drawings. Just as they wanted to be accepted by the bullies, they now want to belong to your group of friends because you can do things that they can't, but wish they could".

Without looking up, Robert said, "My Momma hates me; I don't want her to see my drawings."

Pinky said, "There's no way to keep her from finding out of your coming and that your drawings will be on display. You don't have to talk to her if you don't want to, but by learning of your talent and actually seeing it, might help her understand what she gave away. Maybe you can find comfort in that."

Robert sat for a long time, completely silent, finally, without saying a word, squeezed Pinky's hand and walked away.

Kitty finally came and went straight to Robert, took him by the hand and lead him to the drawings. "They're absolutely beautiful Robert," she said, "you have actually impressed my grandfather; he told me he even bought the drawing you did of him."

"People give us money for them." Robert said.

"I know; my grandfather told me to bring him $250.00," she said.

Finally, Robert got the nerve to say, "Kitty, my friend Pepe wants me to come to his graduation and bring some of my drawings to show at his school. What do you think? Some of the people in that school used to laugh and make fun of me. I don't like it when people laugh at me."

Kitty sqeezed his hand and said, "Robert, I assure you, they won't laugh at you now. They will be amazed at what you can do with your hands. It'll make them very happy to say 'I used to go to school with Robert', I think you should do it; take your drawings and be very proud.

Robert, still uncertain of how to talk to Kitty, said, "You make me feel good when you say things to me."

Again she squeezed his hand and said, "Lets look at what you've drawn since I last saw you." He wondered how it would feel to hug Kitty.

Pinky had made a big birthday cake and called everyone together, "Robert doesn't want presents for himself but instead has asked us to buy a nice grave marker for Rocky. If you would like to contribute to that, just see me and I'll get the monument and have it inscribed and placed.

The response was great, more money than was necessary for the purchase was donated.

"Do you want something written on the marker besides 'Rocky'?" Pinky asked Robert.

"What should I put on it?" he asked.

"Well, something like

[HERE LIES MY FRIEND
ROCKY
HE WAS A GOOD DOG]

"I like that Ms Pinky!"

"O.K. Tomorrow, we'll go to the monument store a pick out one you like."

After selecting the monument the man said it would be ready to install in as soon as two days; he would call before coming to install it.

Pinky instructed the man to get in touch with her personally.

"Is this Ms Pinky?" the man asked.

Yes, this is Pinky"

"I have the monument ready, would you like it installed today"

"Yes. Could you give me an approximate time you'll be here and how long it will take for installation?" Pinky asked.

"What time would you like?" the man asked.

"How about 9:00 in the morning?"

"That will be fine and it shouldn't take more than 30-45 minutes for the installation." the man said

"Tomorrow then."

"Robert, you and I have to go to the bank tomorrow to sign some papers. Will you be ready by 8:00 in the morning?" she asked

"Sure." he said.

Pinky and Robert returned the next day to find everything as planned.

They went to the grave immediately to find the beautiful monument with a picture of Rocky sealed in the monument, a large banner which read,

"HAPPY BIRTHDAY TO A GREAT GUY'

Absolutely stunned, Robert stood silent as tears began to well up in his eyes. When he could no longer contain himself, he fell to his knees and wept. Pinky did nothing for a few minutes then walked to him and took his hand and stood him up.

"Is it alright if I hug you?" she asked Robert.

He didn't wait, but took her in his arms and hugged her tightly, "I'm sorry Ms Pinky, I'm so sad because he died, he was such a good friend," he said.

Pinky took her handkerchief and wiped his tears away, looked up and said, "It's O.K. to cry, that helps us deal with sad situations."

It was 2 months 'til Pepe's graduation, much had to be done in preparation for the school display. First, the superintendent had to be contacted to obtain permission for it; adequate means of transporting the art and personnel had to be procured. The pieces had to be selected as well as the number to be taken.

Ironically, news came to the sanatorium, Robert's mother was found dead in her home. She hadn't been seen for several days, finally someone went to her house and found her.

The director told Pinky since she had a close relationship with Robert, he thought she should be the one to tell Robert of her death.

Pinky went to him and said, "Please come with me to the office, I have something to tell you."

"Have I done something wrong?" he asked.

"No, it's something very serious; let's talk about it in the office."

Pinky led the way with a bewildered Robert close behind. "Come in Robert and have a seat"

Robert sat slumped in his chair, "What is it Miss Pinky?"

"Robert we just got word your mother is dead." Waiting a few moments to see his reaction. Robert showed no emotion,

"Do you want us to provide for you to attend her funeral?"

Quickly, Robert responded," I don't want to go to her funeral. She don't like me so I don't like her back."

"I'm terribly sorry for you. It's just that I wonder, if sometime, much later in your life, you might wish you had gone back to see her; are you sure you don't want to go?" She asked.

Robert sat silent for the longest time; Pinky thinking he might be re-considering.

Finally, "Yes I'm sure, I don't want to see her."

"Very well then; again, I'm so sorry."

After leaving the office, Robert went directly to the dayroom and began to draw. Pinky watched him from a distance. When he had finished his drawing, he sat silent for the longest time, occasionally wiping away a tear. Finally she went to him and placed her hand on his shoulder at which he stood and said, "Miss Pinky, will you hug me."

She embraced him and held him close to her for a very long time, feeling his silent sobs.

When she finally released him and looked at the drawing, her breath caught in her throat. Before her was a drawing of a coffin with the most beautiful woman she'd ever seen, dressed in a beautiful white dress, holding a rose across her chest and just a hint of a smile on her lips. Again, Pinky took him in her arms and held him. He offered no explanation for what he had drawn.

Meanwhile more and more people came to the sanatorium: some to buy what was already drawn, some to have their own things drawn, some just to watch Robert at his work. Soon word began to circulate outside the perimeters of the sanatorium. Newspapers, television and other news outlets came to report on the *boy from down the road*. Sales skyrocketed, necessitating the need for an accounting system to be established.

A special staff meeting was called to discuss the situation.

The director called the meeting to order, "Ladies and gentlemen we have reached a milestone here and some changes have to be made. A great deal of money is being generated within the realms of this organization which have nothing to do with its charter or mode of operations. When we learned of this young man's talent and began to allow the development of that talent, I doubt any of us dreamed of his success; however, to say the least, it's fantastic. Since this young man is a ward of the state, he is our charge. However, his income should be his own, therefore becomes his tax liability. The income must be reported."

Pinky rose to say, "We have more than $2500 to be deposited, am I to open an account in my name, Robert's *and* mine, or is there a better set-up?"

After a moment of consideration the director said, "I suggest you set it up in the two names initially, it can always be amended. How well can Robert spell and write his name?"

After brief consideration, Pinky said, "He can do that fairly well; well enough to be recognized. At this time, he would not understand how to write a check and that is something noteworthy. Maybe special attention should be given as we set up the account." pausing briefly, "There will come a time when he will probably want to buy something quite valuable, necessitating supervision. I'm willing to oversee such things as deposits, small purchases, and keeping him some money along; that will help him to learn more about doing business. However, I'm not comfortable with the charge of being responsible for large, single purchases. I suggest we create a committee which would require that committee be consulted when individual purchases exceed a certain amount; that amount may be determined as we proceed."

"I'll get in touch with the legal department and follow their advice. If the committee thing is what we need, let's decide how many are needed and who would serve," the director said.

Pinky said, "I think three would be sufficient, with limits imposed on each of us for the sake of perception by outsiders."

The director rose from his seat, indicating the end of the meeting and said, "Pinky, you get the account set up, I'll get in touch with the legal eagles and we can go from there."

CHAPTER 18

The Graduation

As Pepe's graduation date drew closer, Pinky went to the director and explained the situation to him and said, "I'd like to have a couple or three days to drive Robert back there. It'll take a little time to set up a display of Robert's work; some special arrangements with the school will be needed in order do that. So far, we haven't contacted them with the idea."

"Take whatever time you need, we'll be fine here." the director said.

Pinky went to Robert to discuss the drawings.

"Do you have a preference of drawings you'd like to take?" she asked him.

"Miss Pinky, can I draw the old school and the big tree and the water and the mountain? Would they like that? If they laughed, I'd feel real bad." His eyes revealed his anguish and uncertainty.

Pinky, taking both his hands in hers and said, "Robert, no one will laugh at your drawings; they will be amazed at how good they are. Besides, I'll be right there with you; so draw your picture of the old school and we'll select a few more for display."

Robert took quite a long time at the task, stopping from time to time, seemingly in deep thought. Pinky wondered if drawing the old school brought back those horrible feelings of being tormented by the other kids.

Eventually, he brought the picture to Pinky.

"Robert, that's astounding, it makes me feel like I attended school there; they will be so proud of you and several will want to buy this picture. Would you want to draw extra ones if they wanted to buy them?" Pinky asked.

"Yes I can draw more like that; that's the way the school looked to me."

Pinky sent a letter to the school superintendent, explaining Robert's talent, Pepe's request for him to attend his graduation, and asking if it would be possible to set up the display.

Shortly a letter came:

"Dear Ms. Summers; as you well know, this is a very special day for the seniors. There should be nothing done that would take away from the joy of graduation. Robert Harrel has been mentioned many times in our circle; mostly, concerning his violent nature. Naturally, you can understand our reluctance to grant such a privilege. However, if you can provide satisfactory evidence that we may be assured of his proper behavior while he's here, your request will be granted and assistance in getting set up will be provided."

Pinky went to the director and asked if he would be willing to write the superintendent a letter of assurance.

After reading the letter from the school, he wrote the following:

Dear Sir: May I say your concern for civility during such an event as high-school graduation is well taken. I can assure you, your opinion of Mr. Harrell is not founded on facts. Robert has been here for many, many months and has never shown any signs of violence; quite to the contrary, he's one of the most pleasant people I've ever known. It's true, he is somewhat intellectually challenged but that has not been a factor at this institution. He has the most extraordinary talent I've ever seen. If your concern is based solely on his behavior, I humbly ask you to grant him the privilege of exhibiting his talent before the school.

As was expected, a letter soon arrived, granting the privilege.

The day came to go the school. After arriving in town, securing a room and unloaded the art, they went to the school to arrange the program.

At the principal's office they introduced themselves and explained what had been discussed. The lady led them to the superintendent's office. Once inside she said, "Mr. Rankin, this is Pinky Summers and this is Robert Harrell; you have talked to them previously?"

"Indeed I have! It's a pleasure to finally meet you." Tom Rankin said, as he took her hand; "and this must be the Robert Harrell; your reputation precedes you. I'm anxious to see some of your work; they say it's very good. How was your trip and have you obtained lodging?"

"Indeed we have and the trip was a most pleasant one. We are here for directions as to how to display our drawings without interfering with your program. Maybe a classroom separate from your proceedings, would be the best for everyone." Pinky said.

"First, I'd like to take a look at his work; did you happen to bring some with you?" Rankin asked.

Even tho he tried desperately to be polite, Pinky could detect a sense of skepticism.

"Yes, this is his latest drawing; it's one of the old school where he attended." as Robert presented is picture.

Rankin stared at the picture for a long time, saying nothing. With his mouth slightly open he finally looked at Robert and asked, "You actually drew this?"

"Yes sir, that's the way it looked to me; I hope you like it." Robert said, dropping his head.

"LIKE IT!! I've never seen anything like it, every detail: the dilapidated ole fence, the big tree, there's the old bell pole. Maybe you can explain the hole in the fence?" still gaping slightly.

"It's where Pepe and I crawled through the fence to watch the fish and animals." Robert explained.

"Why the dog? What part did it play in this scene.?"

"That was Rocky, he was my friend; just Rocky and Pepe were my only friends. Rocky died." Again Robert dropped his head as sorrow swept through him.

"I'm sorry Robert," Rankin said, "he must have meant a lot to you."

"Yes sir, he was a good dog."

"Are all of his drawings this good?" Rankin asked Pinky.

"Absolutely! He drew this picture, with that much detail in less than an hour."

"Then I think I have an idea. Let's put the display on the stage. As the students walk up to receive their diplomas, they can get an idea of their quality and after our ceremony you can take the stage and present your program. I assume if more than one person wants to buy the same picture, you could take orders?"

"Certainly. If someone has a picture of something they would like for him to duplicate, he does that also," Pinky said.

Pinky came to Pepe and asked if he would, at the proper time, take the stage and tell of his and Bobo's relationship.

"I'd be happy to do that." he said.

*

"Ladies and gentlemen, my name is Pepe Posey; Bobo and I are friends. We started to school the same day. We were sort of the outcasts of our class: because of Bobo's unusual nature and my crooked legs and funny speech. Bobo was forced to endure most of the harassment, which was sometimes down right cruel. We hold no animosity toward anyone; young people are sometimes cruel without meaning to be. Still, the effect it has on those who are not well received, has a life-long effect on their development. In Bobo's case, it was a double whammy. His own mother wasn't kind to him; she had him committed to the sanatorium because she didn't want him. She declared him a violent person; so violent she was afraid of him. I know my friend; I know him well! Violence has no room in Bobo's heart. The exact opposite is true. He is the most kind and generous person you'd ever want to meet. I can only imagine the agony he's had to endure.

We have remained good friends and stayed in touch all these years. I consider him the best friend I have in the whole world and hope he feels the same about me. I can only imagine the insecure complex that's his and how it has ruled his behavior. When asked to come here tonight and display his work, his greatest fear was that he might be laughed at and not be accepted. As you will soon see, there is nothing to laugh about!

I hope, before you leave here tonight, you have the opportunity to meet Bobo and learn of his true nature and what he really is; not what he has been perceived to be. When you have opportunity to view his work and recognize its quality, you can rest assured, you've seen the perfection in this man's heart. Thank you."

And now, Bobo's adopted Mom, Ms. Pinky Summers.

As she made her way to the podium, Robert's heart was in his throat, *"How will I ever walk on that stage and look at all the people?"* were his thoughts.

"Thank you Pepe for those kind words. We are here tonight to honor the graduates; indeed it's their day. It is appropriate however, that we honor a young man who was once a part of this class. Through unfortunate circumstances, he became detached from familiar surroundings and has been a patient of ours for many years. He came to us utterly crushed and destroyed; cast away by all of society as he knew it and thrown into a whole new group of strangers which he assumed was an even more hostile world. In his mind, his only friend, except Pepe, whom he felt sure he would never see again, was his little dog with which he was allowed to play a few minutes a day. Robert knew nothing about love; about being hugged, holding hands or of any other display of passion. In his mind, he was in a world alone.

We discovered his talent quite by accident. However, there was one person who knew of it long before it was revealed to us; Pepe was the first to see his work. Asked if he could have what he had drawn, Robert agreed only if he would never let anyone else see it. Being the gentleman that he is, Pepe hid the drawing at home; not even his own Mom knew of it until he was discovered by us. That drawing is among those displayed here.

Robert draws from memory, so if you have a subject you'd like for him to draw, if you'll bring him the object, he'll draw it for the same price. The pictures are numbered and cataloged, if more than one of you would like the same drawings, he'll duplicate as an original.

Robert will now come to the stage and you may then commence to come view his work. If you want to buy some drawing, see me to purchase. Thank you."

As Robert began to make his way to the stage, the audience began to stand and applaud and did so for several minutes. Robert just stood looking at Pinky.

Very quietly, Pinky said, "Turn toward the audience and bow slightly."

Robert, in a jerky manner, waved to them.

As they began to come on stage, they first went to Robert and gave him big hugs, "They're beautiful!" many of them said.

Some where, during the proceedings, Gordy came to Robert.

"You don't remember me, I'm Gordy, the one you decked along with two other guys. Old man Fincher gave you a paddling. I actually felt bad about that; I was the one who should have been paddled. I've thought of that many times. I want to ask you to forgive me.

"Shoot, I forgive you, a lot worse things than that happened to me." Robert said.

He offered his hand to Gordy and the two shook hands. "I'd like to have the drawing of the old school house and grounds." Gordy said.

"Just see Pinky." Robert said as the two parted.

Robert turned back to the display and two feet away was George Fincher poring over the drawings. A pang hit his stomach. He quickly turned and walked away. The old feeling of disdain returned with a vengeance. The possibility of seeing Fincher hadn't crossed his mind. Now that he had, some of the old bitterness he'd felt during the hearing, returned. Maybe someday he might overcome that feeling, but not today.

'I'm so glad for you.' 'They are so good.' 'How do you do that?' were some of the remarks the students made. In spite of all his efforts, there was a feeling of resentment still alive, knowing full well there was little genuineness or sincerity in their remarks.

Pinky could see Robert becoming more and more agitated and began to be concerned. Knowing he was in an unfamiliar setting she wasn't sure what might develop.

Maybe Pepe saw something as well, he walked over and put his arm on Robert's shoulder and said, "They like you very much, Bobo, it ain't like it was; they're a different bunch of people. So what if 'Ole' Fincher is prowling around, he ain't nothing. He probably wishes he could do something that good—anything that good. You're my friend and that's all that matters. You're still the best in my book; you were the best before I knew you could draw and you still are. And someday, we're going to climb that ole mountain."

"Pepe, you make me feel good even when I feel bad. I hope you'll always be my friend."

Finally it was over and most of the people had left. All the drawings were sold except the one original; Many ordered, some said they had different things they would send to Robert and have him draw.

CHAPTER 19

They Re-Visit

"Ms Pinky, after we wake up in the morning, can we drive to the old school and look around?" Robert asked.

"We certainly can and if Pepe isn't doing anything he can go with us."

Quickly, Pepe overhearing, said, "I don't have anything to do, can I please go with you?"

Smiling, Pinky said, "We'll have breakfast at 8 o'clock and be on our way at 9."

Windows knocked out, shingles blown off, doors open, rats and squirrels running in and out; the house looked pretty bad. The old tree was still there and looking pretty much like it always did. The old fence was even more dilapidated than it used to be.

"Ms Pinky, this is where I spent my happy hours before I met you. Someday, I want to buy this place and make my home in that school house."

"My! My!, You'll have to sell a lot of drawings to do all that." Pepe said.

With that, Pepe and Robert walked around the old tree, each looked at the other for a moment, "Let's do it." both said at the same time. After crawling through the hole, they sat down and just watched as the water trickled over the rocks.

"One night I dreamed we climbed that old mountain, all the way to the top. We went through a cloud; it was so beautiful! Sometimes we couldn't see each other but we kept going. We finally got to the top and you could see all the valleys and things. I decided to go for a ride on the cloud went right through it and hit the ground! That's when I woke up." Robert said, chuckling.

Finally Pinky had enough of their reminiscing and ordered the boys back through the fence. "We must be getting back, we have a long way to go and it's getting late." she said.

After dropping Pepe off at his home, they began the trip back to the sanatorium. Everyone was anxious to hear of the event so Pinky gave the report:

"We sold all the pictures we took and have many orders for more. Many wanted the picture of the old school; We have 13 orders for that one alone!

Robert was well received but he was very uncomfortable at times. His old principal was there and that disturbed him for a while but Pepe's calm assurance helped him thru it."

CHAPTER 20

The Inheritence

The director told Robert that Clyde wanted to see him as soon as he returned.

"Come in Robert and close the door," Old Clyde said.

Robert became very agitated and fidgety, "Calm down boy, I'm not going to bite you. I have something to tell you. Kitty, her folks and I have made a decision. I have some property in town, it's worth quite a lot of money. We have decided to give it to you at my death. I had it transferred to Kitty when I came here but now we're going to change the will in your favor. Just so you'll know, Kitty has taken such a shine to you, it's no surprise that the idea came from her. What do you think of that?"

"Mr. Clyde, I don't know what to think. I sure thank you and Kitty. I don't know what to say."

Old Clyde, smiling as though he had done something that gave him a lot of pleasure, said, "Don't say anything; that may be the kindest thing I've ever done and I think it's time I did it. Now git out of here and draw something."

Robert left the room not quite understanding what had just happened to him. He found Pinky and told her what Ole Clyde had done.

"What am I suppose to do now, Ms Pinky?"

"You don't have to do anything yet. The property will eventually belong to you but for now you don't have to do anything. That was a very good thing Ole Clyde did."

With a quizzical look Robert said, "He said it was Kitty's idea."

"Kitty has become very fond of you, I think you should discuss this whole situation with her."

For the rest of the day Robert found it hard to concentrate and, as a result, got very little done. *Why had Old Clyde given him property* kept running thru his mind. Maybe when he saw Kitty again, she could tell him.

CHAPTER 21

The Art Dealer

A tall, well dressed man, came to the sanatorium inquiring of Robert,

"I'm Ryan Parker, an art dealer. I'd like to look over your work if you don't mind."

"Ms. Pinky will show you my drawings," Robert said.

"And where will I find Ms. Pinky?" he asked.

"She's in that office over there," indicating the direction he was to go.

As he started that way he met Pinky, "I'm Ryan Parker, I'm looking for a Ms. Pinky."

"I'm Pinky, how can I help you?"

"I'm an art dealer and I've heard of a young man living here that maybe has a very unusual talent; I have seen a couple of pieces that he supposedly did. Could you show me more of his work?"

"Yes Sir, I'll be happy to; come with me to the day room, we have a display set up there." Pinky said.

Parker stood gawking, hardly believing his eyes, "are you telling me this lad drew these pictures?" he asked.

"Yes Sir he did. He has a back log of requests which keeps him busy all day. Come with me, you can see his work as it develops." Pinky said, leading the man back to Robert.

"Do you mind if I watch you draw?" he asked Robert.

"No, I don't mind, I'm about to draw Rocky, he was my dog. Rocky died, he was a good dog." Robert said, the sadness in his voice was still obvious.

He proceeded to draw Rocky, this time he had a side view of Rocky standing, looking straight at Robert with the same smiling gesture. He finished the drawing in a very short time.

Parker stood for several moments, his mouth slightly ajar, looking at the drawing then at Pinky then back to the drawing. "Where did this guy learn to do that." he said finally.

"Come with me, I'll explain." Pinky said, not wanting to be explicit in Robert's presence.

Back in the office, "I'm sure you've noticed, Robert is somewhat intellectually challenged, along with that, when he came here, he had been terribly abused emotionally, we have been able to help him in a lot of ways, but he is very self-conscious still. He didn't learn to draw, that is a God-given thing. We learned of his talent quite by accident."

"Is he, or some one here, able to market his work?" Parker asked.

"Yes, we have a set-up for him, I being the designated manager. What, may I ask, is your interest in him?" Pinky asked.

"As I've said, I'm an art dealer, and this talent is a rare find indeed. I'm prepared to make an offer for the purchase of his work. I will either buy outright, or work on consignment. To speculate, I need to buy at a lower price of course, but you would have your money immediately. If on consignment, we would split the profit equally, but only after it was sold."

"Robert draws from memory; in other words, he has to actually see an item before he draws. Just once is sufficient, if you have a certain thing you want him to draw, just bring the item in or a picture, or replica, and he takes it from there." Pinky explained, watching to see how Parker responded.

Then continued, "When we decided to display his work, we never considered marketing it commercially; none of us know much about the value of art. Our goal for Robert is to help him find a way to provide for himself now and after he leaves this place."

"So long as the quality of his work is as good as it is, here's what I'm prepared to offer: for the smaller ones, 8 ½ x 11 I'll pay $30; for the 16x16 I'll pay $45 and for the 24x30 I'll pay $125. We prefer to do our own framing. I assure you, that's a fair price."

"What do you expect will be your weekly order?" Pinky asked.

"I make a lot of art shows, I expect I could keep him busy," he answered.

"Mr. Parker, that sounds like a fair offer to me, but as for as a commitment, we have a board which regulates this project. I will have to meet with those people before I can give you an answer. If there are drawings on display here that you want to buy today, feel free to do so. Leave me your number and as soon as I can call a meeting we'll decide how to proceed."

"There are 4 or 5 drawings I would like to take today, to show my prospective buyers," Parker said.

"Make your selections and we'll gladly oblige," Pinky said.

After the transaction, Pinky went to the office and related the proposition to the director.

"I feel everyone will be in favor of this but we have to abide by the rules, so call a meeting as soon as they can meet and lets get this thing rolling," the director said.

As was expected, the board gladly approved the sale and Parker was notified. His first purchase, besides the first 5 he bought, consisted of ten 8 1/2 x11, and five 16x16 for a total of $675.00. There were drawings of Rocky, the fox drinking at the creek, Robert's mother, the old school and Kitty.

CHAPTER 22

The Chat With Kitty

Robert was at his drawing desk, so engrossed in his work that he didn't hear Kitty come up. She stood watching him for a few moments, finally said, "You're working entirely too hard. What's say we sit on the porch a while and talk?"

"Kitty! You surprised me. I reckon old Parker can wait a while." he said.

As he rose from his seat, Kitty took his hand and they walked to the front porch. "Let's sit in the swing." she said and this they did. Robert told her of Parker and his offer. "I have to work real hard now, he wants to buy a lot of my drawings."

"How do you know what he wants to buy?' she asked.

"I reckon he don't care; he says he goes to places where they buy and sell drawings, so if they are good ones, people will buy them."

"Robert, I need to talk to you about something. Grandpa has some property up town, I think it's worth quite a bit of money. My family knows of your background and how life seems to have been unfair. We also know of your special problem. Since I'm the only child my folks have, and they are well off and don't need the property, we have decided to give it to you. It has been willed to me at grandpa's death, but we are about to change that. You have become very special to me; even grandpa has come to admire you; believe me, that's something to write home about.'

"I don't know what to say and I don't know what to do.' Robert said.

"You don't have say anything and you don't have to do anything just yet"

"You know I'm not like other people, some people used to laugh at me because I wasn't like them. I don't know why you like me but I'm glad you do. You are so pretty and nice, and you make me feel real good." Robert said, and except for Pepe and Pinky, for the first time in his life, he felt like someone really cared for him.

They sat silent for a long time, slowly swinging, each one engrossed in thought.

Finally Robert said, "Kitty if I get enough money, I want to buy that old school house. I want to fix it up and live there. For a lot of my life, that was the only place where I felt safe and happy. The stream that runs behind the school had such a good sound as it flowed by. Pepe and me are going to climb that old mountain someday."

There was such a contented look on Robert's face as he spoke. Kitty could only imagine how he felt.

"I'll bet you'll have enough money; with what you earn drawing plus the property here." she said.

"When will you be done with school" Robert asked.

"I graduate from high school next year. I think I'm going to go to college. I like to learn and a person can get a much better job if he goes to college." she answered.

"Will you still come to see you grandpa?" he asked

"OH! Sure, I'll come here often to see Grandpa and to see you. I think you are so nice." Kitty said as she patted his arm.

"Hey! You two, it's time for dinner." Pinky announced.

"I have to go now." Kitty said as she rose from the swing.

Disappointed, Robert said, "Ms. Pinky, can Kitty stay and have dinner with us?"

"Why sure she can; we'd love to have her stay. She might get Old Clyde to smile, who knows?"

"Will you stay Kitty, please?" Robert pleaded.

"Well, O.K. but I have to go soon after we eat."

CHAPTER 23

Robert Begins To Learn To Drive

Pinky came to Robert and said, "Robert, lets you and I take a break and sit in the porch for a while.

"I think I'd like that," he said as he put down his drawing equipment. "Kitty and me sat on the porch and talked and it was fun."

"Robert, there's coming a time when you'll want to leave here and get a place of your own. You're making money now but in order for you to live in your own house there are some things you have to prepare for. You'll have to have a car, and in order to have a car, you'll have to learn to drive."

"How will I get a car, Ms. Pinky?" he pondered.

"Well, lets do first things first. Let's see about teaching you to drive. You have to learn the laws about driving. There is a little book that tells you all about that." Pinky said, then hesitantly, "Do you think you can read well enough to learn that?"

"Maybe you could help me," still uncertain about himself.

"I'll have someone bring us the book and we'll begin," she said.

Pinky went to the director and told of her proposal.

"It just so happens, I have one of the books here in the office and you are welcome to use it." the director said, "and I think you have a wonderful idea. We have done wonders for the guy and he has come a long way."

"This may be our biggest challenge yet, but I believe he can learn to drive, and drive safely," Pinky said, "He's so good with his hands"

Pinky sat with Robert patiently while he pored over the driving instructions.

"What do you do if you want to make a left turn? she asked.

"I put my arm straight out."

"What do you do if you want to make a right turn?" she asked

"I stick my arm straight out, bend at the elbow and point to the sky.

"What do you do if you want to slow down or completely stop," she asked.

"I stick my arm out and point to the ground."

"That's very good Robert, I will ask you these same question as we go through the book to make sure you don't forget."

Learning the rules of driving took him away from his drawings and he began to get behind. However, he had filled all the orders from the school and the orders weren't so pressing at the sanatorium which took some of the demand away. He sat in Pinky's car and practiced shifting the gears, pushing in the clutch, the slowly letting it out. Setting the mirror, adjusting the seat, moving the steering wheel from left to right, right to the left, practicing his turn signals.

Back to the book, what to do when approaching an intersection, who has the right-of-way, and speed limits.

Pinky was amazed at how quickly he caught on.

CHAPTER 24

The Phone

Pinky came to Robert and said, "You have a phone call. Have you ever talked on a phone before?"

"No, I don't know how." he said.

"Come with me and I'll show you what to do."

Inside the office, Pinky picked up the phone and told the party to hold on while she gave Robert instructions.

"This is what we call a receiver, you hold it up to your ear and you can hear what the person calling has to say. Then when it's your turn to talk, you speak into this part. Then it's just like if the person is right here face to face with you." Pinky explained. "When you answer the phone, just say, 'hello'. The person who is calling you can hear you like you hear them. Now there is someone on the phone that wants to talk to you, I think you'll know who it is. Now hold this to you ear and say hello."

Very timidly Robert put the phone to his ear, Pinky adjusted it a little, and said, "Hello?

Hello Bobo? This is Pepe; we got a telephone."

"Hello" Robert said again.

"Just talk to Pepe now, just like he was standing here," Pinky explained.

"Hey Pepe, where are you?"

"I'm home, we got a telephone."

"You can hear me from way over there?" Robert asked.

"Sure can! Just like you can hear me."

"Bobo, I'm going to college in a few days, so I'll be gone for a while but when I come home I'll come see you."

"Pepe, I'm learning to drive a car. I haven't actually drove one yet but I know what to do to make a right turn and a left turn and how to stop. I've learned a lot. Someday I'll be able to drive on the street just like everybody."

'Maybe you can buy you a car sometime, you have lots of money." Pepe said.

"If I do, I'll drive over to see you," he said.

"I have to go now, I'll see you sometime." Pepe said and hung up.

Robert just stood there looking at Ms Pinky, "Is he done talking?"

"He said he had to go and he would see me sometime."

"Okay, put the part that you've been holding up to your ear in the thing on the side of the telephone box."

Still looking bewildered, Pinky took the receiver and showed him how to hang up.

"I never talked to a telephone before," Robert said, "That's a good thing."

"We learn new things everyday, but we never learn everything. Learning can be fun."

CHAPTER 25

Old Clyde's Demise

The day came for old Clyde and Kitty to go to the lawyer's office to will the property to Robert. When Pinky went to wake Clyde, he didn't respond. She waited a couple of minutes and tried again. When he didn't respond, she used her key and went in. She called to him but got no response. She checked his vital signs and realized something was seriously wrong. She called the *on staff* emergency personnel, then the ambulance.

The nurse came to his room and said she was afraid Clyde had had a stroke.

Soon the ambulance came and took Clyde to the hospital where the diagnosis was confirmed.

Pinky called Kitty and her parents to tell them of the situation.

They all met at the hospital, anxious to learn of Clyde's condition. As the doctor came toward them, they could tell by the look on his face what to expect.

"The prognosis is not good. He has only a slim chance of survival. Should he survive, he will be, for the most part, a vegetable," the doctor reported.

With Clyde's family, Pinky, Robert and the director standing at his bedside, at 11:03, Clyde departed this life. On his tombstone was written:

HIS BODY LIVED LONG ENOUGH TO BECOME GROUCHY
BUT HIS HEART NEVER QUITE MADE IT

After the funeral, Robert was unable to draw. Pinky had several sessions with him, explaining how and why people die and how those who love them must live their lives without them. He spent a lot of time at the dog kennel and Pinky was sure he was still grieving for Rocky.

"Robert, I have to get back to college," Kitty said, "I've missed some classes already. When we break for the Holidays this fall, we'll go to the lawyer and fix the deed for the property." She gave him a big hug and continued, "I still say you are a handsome dude."

Robert still could not bring himself to hug her back. After she drove away, he stood for a long time with his head down; Pinky was sure he was crying.

In an effort to cheer him up, Pinky asked Robert "How would you like to have a puppy?"

"Rocky's dead," he said.

"There are other dogs that you could learn to love"

"There ain't no dogs like Rocky. He was my friend; I don't want no other dog."

CHAPTER 26

Robert Solos

"Whats ya say we go for your first drive?" Pinky asked.

"You mean you want me to drive?" he asked

"Sure, you knew it had to happen some day—let's do it now."

Making their way to Pinky's car, she said, "Today, we'll just go from one side of the parking lot to the other to see how well you can make the car go."

Seated in the car, Robert pushed in the clutch, turned on the key and hit the starter. *So far so good* thought Pinky.

When the engine started, Robert became very nervous.

"Just take it easy Robert, you can do it; just remember what we learned from the book." Pinky, speaking calmly, "Now before we put the car in gear, I want you to gradually push down on the accelerator."

The engine roared, startling Robert, and he quickly took his foot off the accelerator, "That's too much." Waiting a few moments for Robert to calm down, she continued,

"Now just push down real slow." This time he did much better.

"Now we will try to move the car a little, I want you to push the clutch all the way to the floor, then very slowly put the car in the 1st gear, you've done this many times while practicing." She waited for him to do that. He just looked at her and she could see the doubt in his eyes, "Go ahead, put it in gear, nothing will happen until you're ready"

Slowly, he put the car in gear, "Now without pushing down the accelerator, very slowly lift your foot from the clutch, very slowly."

The car lurched forward and died.

"Start the car again and push in the clutch, put it in gear and let the clutch out, this time very, very slowly, you will feel the car begin to move, then you can continue to take your foot off the clutch."

Gradually, Robert did as he was instructed and actually got the car moving.

"Now we are ready to stop, so we first push in the clutch, then the brakes. Do that now, push in the clutch." He did that, "Now push in the brakes."

Robert push on the brake pedal so hard and the car stopped so abruptly, Pinky almost went into the windshield.

"You did just fine, but don't push the brake so hard next time. Okay, let's do it again."

After working their way across the parking lot, she instructed Robert how to turn the car around. They continued to practice for a couple of hours but didn't accelerate. Pinky continued to teach, each day they would go through the same routine. After many days, as Robert became more confident he was allowed to go faster and learned how to shift on the move.

After several weeks of training, it was time for him to go it alone. Everyone was nervous, including Pinky, but she felt sure he would be alright.

After his solo. Pinky asked, "How would you like to call Pepe and tell him you've learned to drive a car?"

"Can I Ms. Pinky; can I?"

"First, we have to call his mother and find out when he'll be home, but we'll do that right now."

Much to Robert's dismay, Pepe wasn't due to be home until the holidays.

CHAPTER 27

Robert's Disappearance

"Kitty will be coming home soon," Pinky told Robert, "she'll be here for the holidays."

"I'll be happy, I think she's so pretty," he said.

He found it most difficult to concentrate on his drawing for thinking of Kitty.

At last the day came for Kitty to get home and Robert could hardly be still. He kept looking out the window, expecting to see her anytime. When she finally arrived, he ran to the car as she was getting out. As expected, she gave him a big hug and at last he hugged her back.

For the first time, he saw the driver of the car, "Robert, this is Darwin Hanks; Darwin, this is Robert Harrell, the guy I've told you about. He's one of the most talented people you'll ever meet and one of the nicest as well."

The two shook hands, but Robert's heart was not in it.

"Robert, Darwin and I are engaged to be married, I hope you'll come visit us sometime."

He stood stunned for the longest time, then turned without saying a word, ran to his room and locked the door.

Kitty, surprised, ran after him, knocked on his door but there was no answer.

"Robert, what's wrong? Did I say something wrong? Please let me in and talk to you." Kitty said. There was no answer.

Greatly troubled by his actions, Kitty sought Pinky.

"Pinky, I told Robert of mine and Darwin's plans and I think it disturbed him greatly; he seems to have locked himself in his room. Do you think we ought to try and talk to him?"

"What plans are you talking about?" Pinky asked.

"Darwin and I planned to be married."

"OH my, I imagine he is disturbed."

The two went to Robert's room and knocked on the door and called to him but there was no answer.

"Robert, this is Ms Pinky, open the door, I need to talk to you."

Still no answer.

"Robert, open the door."

Still no answer.

Robert, open the door now or I'll open it with my key."

Finally, and very slowly, he opened the door.

"Ms Pinky, you can come in but I don't want Kitty to come in."

"Why don't you want Kitty to come in?"

"'Cause she don't like me no more," he said.

"OH, that's not true, she likes you very much; have you forgotten the gift?"

"I don't care about the gift, I liked Kitty and now she likes someone else. I don't want to be here any more. I don't want to draw anymore, I want to go to the old school house and see the big tree and hear the water and the wind; maybe

I'll climb the mountain. I don't want to be here anymore. Ms Pinky, will you hug me?"

Pinky, not knowing how to handle the situation, simply took him in her arms and held him. His whole body was trembling. Neither said anything for a long time.

"Ms Pinky, will you take me back to the old school house? Please!" Robert said.

"Yes I will, but let's wait a few days until you feel better," she added, hoping by then the shock will have worn off.

"Ms Pinky, I'm never going to feel better; please can you take me, just for a day?"

"Okay, tomorrow morning I'll take you there for one day and then you have to come back. Okay?"

Robert just nodded.

Next day as they arrived Robert said, "I want to be here alone today, can you just leave me here 'til later?"

"Okay, but I'll be back long before sundown, will you be ready then?"

He shrugged his shoulders and she left.

Later, Pinky came back only to learn that Robert was no where to be found. She called to him several times but there was no answer. Not knowing what else to do she went to the police station and told the story.

The officer said, "I'll go take a look; maybe he didn't hear you call."

Using the station's phone, she also called the sanatorium and reported the situation.

"He'll probably show up Pinky" the director said, "Just give him a little more time. If not, let me know and we'll get some people to help look for him."

"There's not much to go on here. He evidently spent some time here against this tree, you can see the tracks of his shoes; it looks like he has crawled through the fence for some reason," the officer said. "Do you suppose he might have gone up the mountain?"

"That's a good possibility, he has mentioned that he wanted to climb it someday." Pinky said.

"Well, it's getting dark and there's little we can do 'til morning; maybe he'll show up." the officer said wistfully.

Again, Pinky went to the police station and called the director, "We haven't been able to find him, the officer says there's nothing we can do until morning. Do you have any suggestions?"

"Do you think he's on the mountain?" he asked.

"Right now, I think that's the best guess. If so, what do we do?" she asked.

"I'm with the officer, if he doesn't show up on his own, there's nothing that can be done until we are able to see. If that's the case, we should organize a search party in the morning," he suggested.

Feeling the impact and responsibility for the whole situation, Pinky said, "I'll go back to the school and sit in my car in case he does show up; I'll check with you in the morning."

Except for the scurrying sound of nocturnal animals and an occasional hoot from an owl, the night was quiet and very, very long for Pinky.

Pinky drove back to the station and reported.

"I think we should get some people together and begin to look for him," she said.

"Very well, I'll call in the volunteer firemen and we'll begin," the officer said.

Again Pinky called the director, "There was no sign of Robert last night, we are in the process of assembling a search party now. Do you have any suggestions?' she asked.

"For now, let's let the authorities handle the search. I probably should not leave here just yet, you can handle matters quite well and I'll be available if you need me," the director said.

The officer directed the 8 men, "4 of you go up stream 15 minutes and 4 down stream fifteen minutes, if you find something, report back sooner, if not, come back to base and we'll start the up hill search.

35 minutes later the 8 men reported back; no results.

"Take a 10 minute break, looks like this might be a long drawn-out affair," the officer advised. We'll go up as far as we can in 2 ½ hours, if we don't find him, we'll come back down. You have to pace yourself, this is a steep mountain and a tedious mission we are on. Keep 30 feet between you, everyone stay in line. After fifteen minutes, stop and take a breather; occasionally call out.

*

For a long time he sat leaned back on the old tree. Memories poured back like rain: *The first time he saw Rocky; the way he always met him in the mornings as he got to school, The many times he and Pepe sat and watched the little fish in the water and the sound it made as it flowed by. Memories of the way the kids treated and made fun of him and the memories of how Pepe was always his friend, even when the others were so hateful. Then there was old man Fincher but I don't want to think about him.*

If I'm ever going to climb this old mountain, now is as good a time as I'll have. No one cares if I climb or not; no one cares. Pinky says she cares but she probably don't. Kitty said she cared but she don't. Only Pepe cares for me and I don't know where he is.

The sound of the stream flowing by and the wind moving the trees raised his determination and he crawled through the fence and started toward the top.

His thoughts continued. *I don't know if I can get to the top today but I don't care, I'll just keep on going tomorrow. Nobody cares anyway. Kitty said she cared and that I had a pretty smile but she didn't mean it. She is so pretty, I wish she liked me.*

He soon became tired and stopped to rest, but the thoughts wouldn't stop:

I bet old Gordy was lying when he ask me to forgive him, he probably didn't care if I forgave him or not.

He fell asleep and when he woke up he realized it was colder the farther up the mountain he went.

I wish Ms Pinky would go back to the sanatorium and not tell anyone where I am. They just want me to draw things for them anyway. I don't want that old stuff that Old Clyde and Kitty gave me, I just want to get to the top of this mountain.

*

At the first break, they all came together, "Anyone find anything?" the officer asked.

No one said anything.

"Then we'll continue on to the next break. Be sure you take some water often."

As was planned Pinky called the director. "Do you know anymore about Robert; any definite idea of his where-abouts?" he asked Pinky.

"No we don't. They are now climbing the mountain in hopes of finding him or some sign that he's really up there."

When the director hung up the phone he turned to find Kitty listening intently. "Have they learned anything of Robert?" she asked.

The director shook his head and said, "Nothing yet."

"I feel so terrible, all this is my fault. I had no idea his learning of my engagement would upset him this way," Kitty said.

"He's a very special person, his emotional situation is such, that he's unable to deal with disappointment. This is not your fault," the director assured her."

Pinky called Pepe's mom and asked if he was home.

"No, he not here but he's expected to be later on today. They're coming home for the holidays." she said.

"Could you tell him that Robert is missing and we are at the old school house while they search the mountain for him. I think he will want to know." Pinky said, "If all goes as planned, they'll come down from the mountain around 3 o'clock this afternoon. I'd appreciate it if you could bring him down here. He knows Robert better than anyone, maybe he could help us find him."

Pepe came about the time the men returned from looking for Robert with no results. No sign was found.

"I wonder if he's even on the mountain," one said.

"Bobo's dream was to climb that mountain someday, I bet he's up there somewhere," Pepe said. "He told me once about a dream he had of getting to the top and how beautiful it was and how far you could see. He and his dog started to climb it one time and were out all night. They might have been in trouble that time if it weren't for his dog."

Everyone agreed to meet the next morning to try again. Hopefully, there would be others that would come help with the search.

*

I'm cold and hungry but I'm going to get to the top before I quit. I must be close.

Trudging along, he was finally compelled to stop for rest.

The wind had begun to blow, making the cold even more bitter. Finding a cave like recess under a rock, he sat down to rest, nearly exhausted.

His thoughts turned to Pinky, *I bet Ms Pinky is mad at me; I hope she ain't, I think she really likes me.*

He soon fell asleep and didn't wake until it was daylight. He was so cold he could hardly move. Looking back down hill, it was tempting to go back. The thought came to him, *To what?*

So he turned upward, shivering but determined, trudging toward the top. His hands and toes were numb, but he was gaining heat as he went along. Finally it came to one of two choices: become too tired to go any further or be too cold to rest.

His steps became harder and harder, finally he was forced to stop and again fell asleep.

When he awoke it was so foggy he couldn't tell uphill from downhill, he couldn't feel his toes or his fingers and when he tried to get up, he stumbled and fell. Try as he would, he could not get to his feet. He crawled to a small tree but his hands were so cold he could not grip it.

Maybe if I rest a little more, I can do it.

The longer he lay there, the sleepier he became and soon began to get warm. Kitty was there reassuring him of her love for him. Looking up, he saw Rocky running toward him at full speed and was soon in his arms; there they were together again. Sadly, he never got to tell Pepe he learned to drive a car.

CHAPTER 28

The Discovery

The search for him went on for 4 days and was eventually called off. Pepe was nearly hysterical, "We can't quit looking for Bobo, we can't!"

"Son we've done all we can, there's no assurance that he's even up there," the officer said. "Besides, there is a good chance some of the searchers could fall prey to this old mountain."

Pinky called the director and gave him the news. "Well, we have to continue the search for him. There must be someone around there who has horses that could be used to get closer to the top of the mountain."

"I'll ask around," Pinky said and hung-up. Turning to the officer she asked, "Are there people around here who have horses we might use to continue the search, allowing us to get closer to the top,"

"Yes ma-am, that might give us more information if nothing else."

Pepe chimed in, "I don't know how to ride a horse but I could ride behind someone, I believe I can help find him."

Next morning, two men with horses came to the school house and the fence was cut for access to the mountain, Pepe aboard, they began their journey uphill.

"Me and Bobo started to climb this old mountain one day but we didn't get very far before it got late and we had to come back down. We went right up that way," indicating the direction for the rider to go.

Occasionally they stopped to rest the horses. Soon they found themselves in fog so thick they could hardly see. "Here's where we'll find him, he always wanted to ride on a cloud. I believe if we look real good in this fog, we'll find him," Pepe said.

For the next half hour they rode around in the fog.

"There he is!" the rider yelled, "Right over there."

Still partially holding to the little tree, was the body of Robert Harrell.

Pepe bailed of the horse and ran to him, "Bobo! Bobo! Wake up Bobo! Please don't be dead Bobo! One of the riders took his arm and said, "He's dead son."

Pepe fell to his knees and sobbed uncontrollably for several minutes. Finally one rider said to the other, "We can tie him on my horse and take turns walking back down."

After regaining his composure Pepe said, "I know it's a very big thing to ask of you, but Bobo so wanted to get to the top of the mountain, could you just go a little further? Maybe we aren't far from the top."

One rider looked at the other; neither spoke; finally one shrugged his shoulders and began to lead Bobo's horse toward the top.

Shortly they were out of the fog and found they were above the tree line although not to the top of the mountain.

As they sat, giving the horses a breather, Pepe came to the body of Robert and said, "Bobo, we've brought you to the top of this old mountain; it's so beautiful; even more than we thought. We are now going to go back through the that old fluffy cloud you always wanted to ride on, but this time when you go through it, you won't hit so hard."

For a few moments Pepe just stood with his hands on Bobo; his grief was obvious.

They then began their journey downward.

CHAPTER 29

The Conversation

Kitty, I'd like to talk to you," Pepe said, "they have asked me to deliver the eulogy at Bobo's funeral. I want to speak of how and why Bobo did what he did. Bobo's dead and if you don't feel comfortable with me speaking as I want to speak, I'll approach it another way. I know you feel responsible for his death but that's not true; it's much, much deeper than that. Bobo came into this world, not as a bundle of joy but as a malignancy that was removed from his mother's womb. She, instead of being happy, was repulsed at the sight of him. In addition to all these things, they were compounded by retardation. If you can imagine that, then you have a start at understanding my friend. Until he was 6 years old he might as well have been marooned on an island by himself. He knew nothing of love, of belonging to something, or what it meant to have friends with which to share secrets and personal likes or parents to tell him what he could and couldn't do. You and I can't imagine such a state of mind. He knew nothing of trust. He was leery of everybody. He had heard the neighbors laughingly say, "Here comes Myrtle's Wonder—wonder who his daddy is?" He had heard the jeers of the kids at school, he learned of injustice by those having authority, to him that was what life is all about.

It was only when we started to school that he began to know about friends.

I was the only person on this earth that cared about him and wanted to be his friend.

Later Rocky came into his life and for the first time, he had something that truly loved him and showed it constantly. Since he was unable to tolerate the way people treated him at school, he simply quit and put all his confidence and affection on Rocky and me. I was unable to be around him often because of school activities. In his mind there was only he and Rocky. When his mother was hurtful to Rocky, he tried to protect him. His mother saw an opportunity to get rid of both of them for good—and did.

The best break he ever had was when he came to the sanatorium. Ms Pinky did wonders for him. He learned to love; he learned how to let others love him back, he learned how to trust people. When his talent was eventually revealed and people began to appreciate what he could do, I believe he was finally beginning to shed that awful self image. I believe you were the first *special* person in his life. Surely you can take some comfort in that. Because you didn't share the same feelings and in the same way, he felt a disappointment with which he was unable to deal.

Can you imagine dealing with uncertainty and having no one to turn to for advice?

Kitty, you and I have parents in whom we may confide; people with whom we may share our problems and disappointments and expect reassurance and gain confidence; Bobo had no one."

Kitty sat sobbing, "I loved him so much!"

Pepe continued, "There's a song with a line, **'Love is a Many Splendored Thing'**. We love many different things and each <u>love </u>is different: we love our parents, our pets, our friends, our country; the line is endless. The love you have for Darwin is a very special love. There is no love like it and you should not have to apologize or feel guilty.

There is something about this tragic event in which I believe we may find some comfort. Most of us have dreams and usually live a lifetime endeavoring to fulfill those dreams. Bobo's dream was two fold: one was to climb that old mountain and the other was to ride on a cloud. I believe he fulfilled those dreams with his final journey."

Pinky had stood nearby throughout Pepe's talk with kitty.

"Pepe, that was good; Kitty will never forget this event no matter how long she lives, but you have given her a way to cope with the memory of it. Thank you." Pinky then went to Kitty and held her 'til she stopped crying.

Darwin was the perfect gentleman through it all. Finally, when everyone had had their say and done their thing, he went to Kitty and took her hand, "We'll deal with it, I'll always be here for you," then took her in his arms.

CHAPTER 30

Later, after everyone had regained their composure, Pinky came to Kitty, "Do you feel like talking?"

"Yes, I'm alright, and thank you for helping me through this."

"I'd like to discuss something with you. Robert has several thousand dollars in the bank; it's in my name. Robert expressed a desire to buy that old school house and fix it up to live in. I don't have a real good idea what it will cost to do that, but if there's not enough money in my account, I would like to ask you, if you would consider selling the property that was about to be given him and put it toward the purchase of the property? Since that's the place where he felt most comfortable, I'd like to have him buried by the old tree." Pinky said.

"With my blessing! What a great idea! Let's get that done immediately, if the landowner will agree, we'll have him buried there and we can complete the transaction later. We should get a great monument as well. I would like to write his epitaph." Kitty said.

At the funeral, Pepe delivered the eulogy explaining what is perceived to be the thing which precipitated Roberts action, concluding, "I believe he has found the peace and love now, that eluded him in this life."

After the eulogy, and as the people passed the coffin to view the body, many lay a single rose on the coffin; others touched his hands; some simply touched the coffin. Kitty was the last to walk by. No one had noticed what she held in her hand. After standing for a few moments she placed the drawing Robert had done of her on his chest with this inscription:

> ***I GO WITH YOU AND I'LL BE YOUR***
> ***VALINTINE FOREVER.***
> ***I LOVED YOU DEEPLY. KITTY***

And so it was. The landowner, as it turned out, was a customer of Robert's and readily agreed to have Robert buried on the property. He would take no money for it but stipulated : the property must be fenced, the old building renovated, made into a museum where Robert's work would always be displayed.

CHAPTER 31

Preparatons For
The Musuem

Word spread rapidly of Robert's demise, many came to offer their condolences. As people learned of the impending project, some offered to display their drawings.

This possibility was brought up for discussion at the staff meeting.

After Pinky explained these offers, the director said,

"We have to form an entity, give it a name, *it* being responsible for subsequent matters which might arise. That necessitates the appointing of officers. As for those offering to have their works displayed, constitute a question of ownership: do they want to donate their drawings or loan them? If they should want to retain ownership, special arrangements must accompany their material."

Pausing, waiting for questions or comments; none were offered and the director continued. "Since the money earned while Robert lived will be donated to this project, I assume it may be considered a charity donation, therefore will have no tax liability."

Turning to one of the board members, the director said, "Jack, I want you to contact our legal guys and have them put together whatever it is we need."

"Yes sir."

Back to the director, "Is there any reason why we can't begin the project of renovating the building?"

"I know of none," Pinky volunteered, "We have to do first things first. We'll need to meet with an architect and get ideas for laying out the floor plan. I can get in touch with one and have him look and give us ideas."

"Let's make that our next step," the director said, "All originals should be permanently frozen but provision could be made for selling duplicates, that income might be used for maintenance.

CHAPTER 32

Pinky and Kitty went to the monument company to select the headstone.

Meanwhile, Kitty had composed the epitaph and gave it to the stone mason,

"It will have to be a very large stone in order to get that much information engraved on it," he said.

"It doesn't matter, the inscription must be there, also there is a drawing of Robert that must be attached to the stone," Pinky said.

"After selecting the stone the man said he should have it ready for installing in about three weeks.

"Could we have the installation delayed until we dedicate the overall project?" Kitty asked.

"Of course. We'll be ready when you are."

A year passed and the celebration was planned to coincide with the holiday break for the college students. Finally, after the closing on the property, the architect's work, the renovation of the building was completed and display racks, special lighting, and the displays of hundreds of Robert's drawings in place, the building was ready for the opening. Those items which were donated were inscribed, "*Donated by____*.

The head-stone was delivered and installed with the drawing of Robert at his easel. It was then tarped, awaiting the ceremony.

In the center of the gallery, encased in glass was the message:

Robert Harrel was born August 26, 1929

He was considered to be intellectually challenged and for many years, rejected by society.

Even his mother despised him and lied in order to get him committed to a sanatorium where his talent was discovered.

He drew from memory or as an object appeared to him. The drawing of himself that you see on his tombstone was done as he sat before a mirror. He did this at the behest of the many who knew him.

His tragic and accidental death occurred as he endeavored to fulfill a dream of climbing the mountain behind you and riding on one of the fluffy clouds.

Pepe was responsible for getting the word to all those from the old school who might be interested in attending the affair. The monument company was asked to have all the preliminary work done so the unveiling of the monument might be the center part of the celebration. Pepe agreed to be the keynote speaker with Kitty the Master of Ceremony.

Finally the day came for the Grand Opening of

The
ROBERT HARRELL
ART DISPLAY

Kitty rose and brought the assembly to order and gave an outline of the planned agenda.

She explained the means of buying some of Robert's work, "We cannot sell the original drawings, but if you would like to obtain a duplicate of a favorite, see the person at the desk to my left and she'll give you the details. Pepe has a few remarks, after which we'll have the unveiling of the tombstone. Ladies and gentlemen, Mr. Pepe Posey."

Pepe's delivery:

"Thank you ladies and gentlemen; Bobo would be pleased with this day.

I've been asked to say a few things about the person being honored here today.

I like to think I was his closest friend. He and I have shared many things together. We had great plans for our adult life and spent many hours watching the wild-life behind the fence. Bobo was special and was born to a mother that loathed him from his birth, she was very negligent and abusive; he was borne into a world in which he didn't readily adapt, so it was a natural thing for him to turn to animals for companionship.

Some describe Bobo's condition as 'retarded'; the profundity that was his, and is displayed before you, enables one to know the term 'retarded' doesn't really apply to him.

Bobo had a big heart, but he had only a very few people with which to share. He had the greatest capacity for love, but only a very few whom he could love and have it reciprocated. The heart and soul of this man was as pure as his work.

One of his earliest dreams was to climb this old mountain behind me; that dream never left him.

Another dream he had was to ride on one of those fluffy ole clouds he spent lots of time admiring. In his mind, the fulfillment of these dreams would provide the ultimate sanctuary. I like to think in his final day, he fulfilled both and obtained the peace that constantly eluded him in this life.

A later dream of his was to buy this old school-house and convert it into a dwelling. It seemed to those of us, who were close to him, to be appropriate to make this his final resting place."

After pausing for a moment, he continued,

"Now let's move to the grave site for the unveiling of the tombstone."

As the tarp was pulled away, there were oohs and ahhs from the crowd. The beauty of the stone was compelling, but the thing that drew the greatest awe and admiration was the drawing of Robert at his easel.

Etched below the picture was the epitaph:

ROBERT HARRELL
August 26, 1929-December 4, 1946

In the course of life, one will meet many:
Some become friends, some enemies:
Most will be mere acquaintances.
On some rare day one may meet that special
person:
One who fits into a category all his own
His unique characteristics set him apart from all
others
Such was the great guy who rests here

FROM THOSE WHO KNEW AND LOVED HIM

Epilogue

After the ceremony was finished and everyone went their way, Pinky went to back the sanatorium and to her desk. Almost completely exhausted physically and emotionally, she took pen and paper and began to write a letter to Robert:

To my son Robert: the son I always wanted but never had.

You once asked me if I would be your Momma. That question seemed to me to be inappropriate. I should have been asking you if I <u>could</u> be your Momma. I took pride in your accomplishments such as only a mother could have in a child. You brought me happiness that I shall never have for anything again. Rest well, you'll always be in my heart.

Folding the paper, she put it in her special place, along with a drawing of an angel.